Aerom

Ahquabi House Publishing
11872 G58 Hwy
Indianola, IA 50125

ISBN: 978-1-387-76032-9

The First 91

After Orville Wright made his first powered flight in 1903, he and his brother, Buzz, who flew second, returned to their home airport in Dayton, Ohio, where they put their names on the hangar waiting list and for the next thirty-two years hung around the pilot's lounge retelling their flying story. In 1967, I took my first flight in an Air Force C-130 Hercules, and, without spoiling the plot (that story appears on page 148), I began to stockpile my own flying stories. Point is, all pilots are storytellers, because we all have adventures to share. Or as Buzz Wright said in 1904, when being interviewed by Terry Gross on NPR for the first anniversary of flight, "Anyone can be first, but only those who follow number one can bear true witness to history as we interpret it." [1]

The aviation clubhouse is packed with more flying stories than stars over Hollywood. This collection holds 91 of mine, written in the 32 years between 1981 and 2014. When you add up 91, 32, 1981 and 2014, without using a calculator, the sum is anything you want it to be. Same with telling flying stories. Reality loses function when it arrives on wings.

Each story in this volume is based on some aspect of aviation I've experienced, either as a fledgling private pilot, ramp rat, flight instructor or from my years as an air traffic controller. They're all fantasy plucked from the garden of self-editing memory and reflect how I feel about this romantic thing called flight.

Some of these stories appeared in Pacific Flyer magazine (Wayman Dunlap, publisher/editor) and Minnesota Flyer (Richard Coffey, publisher/editor). Many appeared on my audio books, Ailerona and The Logbook.

Aeromancy Volume 1 would never have made it out of computer memory had not Karey Sanderson shown me how to actually retrieve them from old floppy discs...actually, she tried to show me but realized that it was easier to do the layout herself. She also designed the cover. Student pilots who've suffered through my whiteboard illustrations know that I lack Karey's artistic talents.

---

[1] Ed. Note: Berge is making that up about the Wright Brothers. He does that and should be stopped.

If there's one story in this collection that motivates you to head to the airport for the sole purpose of taking in the infinite romantic possibilities of defying gravity, then Aeromancy has succeeded.

Enjoy, fly often and write when you find words.

—Paul Berge
Ailerona, Iowa USA
March 31, 2017

Chapter 1
Airport Kids

"Hey, Kid"

Nowhere is hotter than New Jersey in August. But in 1967 one 13-year-old boy with sunburnt pimples and unruly hair escaped the heat by pedaling to Teterboro airport. There, he'd sit in the shade of a derelict Twin Beech and imagine where each departing airplane was headed. That Stinson 108 lifting off might be bound for Maryland. Or the Lockheed Lodestar taxiing past the control tower could be hauling mobsters to Maine. The airplanes flew wherever his imagination allowed.

All summer he'd ride the perimeter road and lock his bike to the FBO's fence. Ignoring KEEP OUT signs he'd climb over and drop to the other side like a paratrooper onto an island of civility. Outside, the noise of trucks, freight trains and sirens intensified the sulfurous urban heat. But within airport boundaries propellers cleansed the air to make pilots look cool. He'd never flown but knew how to dream. More importantly, he'd learned to wander the rows of parked airplanes without adult interference. Until one miserably hot day when someone shouted, "Hey, kid!"

Such a phrase was usually followed by "Get the hell outa there!" But this voice came from a pilot standing on a Bonanza wing. His shiny head dripped sweat onto a floral red aloha shirt clinging to him like Saran Wrap. An unlit cigar butt poked from the corner of his mouth. "You wanna make a few bucks?" In New Jersey an offer like that might involve disposing of something unpleasant in the Hudson River. But before the kid could answer, "What do I gotta do?" the pilot waved him over and pointed to a bucket. "Ever wash an airplane?"

"Sure," the kid squeaked. The pilot suspected he was lying but grinned and said, "Great. I'll unroll the hose."

Cities can build all the water parks they want, but nothing refreshes the soul better than washing an airplane on a hot day. And nothing captures a future pilot quicker than hearing the owner say, "Gotta dry it off. Wanna fly?"

Kids are warned to never accept money or rides from strangers, but this one took both. His sneakers were still wet when the airplane lifted off and tucked its gear into the wells. He was amazed how close the New York City skyline was and how strong it looked against the hazy sky. When he saw the Atlantic Ocean sprawling to infinity, he mumbled, "I had no idea it was that close..."

4

The airport kid became a flyer, another human who could never again feel completely at home on the ground. Now, forty-plus years later, he lives on the opposite coast and still feels uneasy on the planet. So, whenever temperatures climb he and his wife ride bikes to the airport, roll their Bonanza from the hangar and look for any excuse to wash it. Then, when they're both thoroughly soaked, she'll pull him close and whisper in her Lauren Bacall voice, "Hey, kid, ever been flying?" And the 13-year-old airport kid in him reemerges.

"Aerial Geometry"

"The shortest distance between two points is, what?" A collective blank stare on twenty faces met the teacher's question. "This is basic geometry, class, and will be on the exam." He sighed. "What is the shortest distance between two points?"

"Up," Louise replied softly while staring out the window. Up was the unit separating the fifteen-year-old at her earthbound desk from a small airplane crawling across the spring sky. The teacher thought her a dolt, but given that hers was the only response in a roomful of mummies, he pressed on. "Not exactly, Louise, but, let's say your desk is point A…" He drew a large dot on the chalkboard and labeled it A. He then traced a squeaking track to a higher dot and marked it B. "And here in the sky is…"

"A Cessna 195," Louise interrupted and pointed to the teacher's B. "It's an airplane with a radial engine, carries five, cruises 148 knots. That's what I saw flying across the sky."

"Fine," the teacher answered slowly and sketched a crude airplane beside the letter B. "If we connect A to B we see that the shortest distance between them is a straight line." The chalk broke as he tapped the airplane.

"But it's no longer there."

"What's no longer there?"

"The airplane—B. It moved, flew on, escaped from being anywhere; that's what airplanes do." And before the teacher could jump in, Louise continued, "Besides, there are no straight lines in flight."

"Nonsense, Louise. What about the wings? They're straight."

The girl was already shaking her head, no. "Curved," she said and held her arms out. "Allows air to flow across and produce lift. Plus, the tips are round, and if you look carefully you'll see that wings twist ever so beautifully. They only seem straight to those who can't see enough to fly."

By then Louise was swooping around the classroom, her arms arched and banking. One by one the other students caught the grace in her movement, opened their numbed minds and felt lift tug them from their seats.

"But what about the routes the airplanes fly?" the teacher protested as Louise floated past with toes barely skimming the floor. "They must follow a line across the map from Point A to Point B!"

"But the world is round, and the sky has no shape," Louise answered with a smile as she drifted onto the ledge of an open window. "Lines are only in your mind, Mr. Burns. You can't believe in them and fly." And with that she soared out the window and across the schoolyard, knocking the hat off a school superintendent. And before the administrators could shut the window, the entire class took to flight and was free.

Wham!

Louise woke from the crack of a Geometry textbook slapping her desk. Mr. Burn's breath smelled of stale cigarettes as he leaned into her and growled, "You'll never amount to anything, Miss Louise." And he was right. She became a pilot instead.

© 2011

"Airport Bum(s)"

Sky—there's nothing like it on earth. To Briana, 17, the sky was the one place that made the planet bearable. Or at least that's how she felt as she climbed from the Citabria and ran her fingers through shaggy red hair. Her scalp itched where the headset had been clamped through an hour of loops, rolls and spins. She squatted, lay back in the wing's shade on the damp grass and groaned, "It's so unfair."

Like many teenagers, Briana was on the wrong planet; this one had way too much gravity. She belonged to the 3-D sky and dreaded returning to earth and school with its one-dimensional thought. How could she sit among rows of dull minds while hers was slicing a wingtip through cumulus clouds? Dissecting Wuthering Heights paled when reliving the summer day she'd landed on a high desert road just to feel the heat. As others fretted over base 8 math problems, Briana stepped her mind through Cuban 8s.

She glanced at her watch—7:37. Classes began at 8:10, and each morning she'd stop by the airfield to spend a few minutes in her sky before placating reality. Today, she couldn't find the strength to get up. Didn't try real hard, either and, instead, closed her eyes, "Just for a minute," she muttered before falling asleep.

It'd be nice to think she dreamed of flight, but the truth is, she just slept. Snored, too, until the slow clack of an engine made her turn and face a figure wrapped in light. She twisted onto an elbow and shaded her eyes. "Are you…" she hesitated, because this sounded really implausible, "An angel?" The silhouette answered in a deep voice thick with New Jersey insight: "Heck no, lady. I'm just tryin' to cut the grass and nearly ran over ya. Stopped to see if you was dead or somethin'"

Briana stood and smacked her shoulder on the wing strut. The stranger shook his head, and when he turned away she saw that he was only slightly older than her. He climbed onto a small diesel tractor that idled nearby and reached for the lever to spin the mower blades. "Why ain't you in school?" he asked.

"Because it's boring," she thought but, instead, replied, "I was just going…"

"No you wasn't," he countered. "You was playin' hooky."

"Was not…"

"Wanted to, though, didnchya?" He smiled, and she grinned in return.

"Yeah, I think about quitting every day."

"And do what, become an airport bum like me?" She liked the idea, but he cut her off with, "You couldn't make it as a bum." And he engaged the mower, so she had to shout over the whir: "I can do anything I put my mind to!" And she awoke 20 years later in the shade a flight school hangar beneath a sign that read: Dr. Briana's Sky—No Place Like It On Earth. And as her husband pushed their Citabria out, she said, "Told you I could make it."

© 2008

"The Walk-In"

Ace hunched over his workbench inside a small shop in the hangar's southwest corner. Greasy sunlight oozing through a four-pane window flooded the disassembled magneto on the bench. He squinted behind reading glasses at the end of his nose while trying to set a tiny screw into the points.

"Excuse me," a young voice interrupted, and the screw popped off the magneto and onto the floor.

"Gadflabbidy blast!" Ace hissed and turned like an old turtle about to snap a minnow. "See what you did?"

The teenager hadn't. He stood awkwardly, half in shadow and shifted from one sneakered foot to the other before asking, "Are you the flight instructor?" Ace stared at the walk-in who pressed on, "I wanna learn to fly."

"Why?"

"I don't know." Shrug. "Just seems like something I gotta do."

"You have a name?"

"Brian."

"How old are you?"

"Eighteen." Then: "Seventeen...almost."

"Have any money?" the old instructor asked. Brian nodded, yes, but Ace mumbled that he'd probably need more. Brian stood undeterred with the resilience of a dream that refuses to wake. Ace spotted the missing screw and, reaching down for it, said, "Get the broom." He pointed. "Let me know when you're done sweeping out the hangar." And he turned back to the workbench.

An hour later, Ace stood where Brian had piled a sizable mound of junk and was scooping it into a bucket. "Don't throw that out," Ace growled and waved Brian toward a countertop along the wall. Ace ducked beneath a Cessna 170's wing strut, took the bucket and dumped the contents. Running his fingers through the dirt he picked out a bolt. "See? Perfectly good hardware," he said and dropped the AN bolt into a coffee can. "Bolts go in that one, screws there and washers in here." Ace indicated various cans on a shelf. "Call me when you're done." And then grumbled, as he turned away, "Can't just walk in here thinking you can throw money out and expect to fly."

It was late afternoon when Ace showed Brian how to preflight, start and taxi the Cessna. In their hour aloft Brian saw for the first time how immense the world really was. After landing he spent another hour wiping down the airplane and rereading his first logbook entry. And it took all summer before the hangar was completely swept, allowing the walk-in to fly out alone.

Thirty-three years later, Brian squinted at a disassembled magneto on the workbench in the hangar's southwest corner. He was about to set a tiny screw into the points when someone knocked on the doorframe.

"Gadflabbidy blast!" Brian swore and swiveled to find a teenager standing there. "What?"

"I wanna learn to, like, fly. Are you, like, the instructor?"

Brian sighed. "Do you want to fly or to 'like' fly?"

The young man stared until Brian said, "Grab the broom…" And then, "Got a name?" The walk-in turned as he picked up the broom and grinned before answering, "Just call me Ace."

© 2011

"Betty Bounce"

It's impossible to forget your first love. The time, the place, and especially the aroma of obsession imbeds itself inside the brain, and years later you can be on another planet when a mere whiff of fragrance will trigger the sweetness of memory and, in my case, a memory lost.

She was a Cessna 195, and I fell in love with her one cold Saturday when I'd ridden my bicycle out to watch airplanes take off and land. My friends thought me just shy of nuts for wasting time staring at flight, but they hadn't yet felt love, didn't know its velvet grasp. At 14, I was captive. It had begun innocently enough when I'd slipped through the chain link fence at New Jersey's Teterboro Airport to walk the rows of parked aircraft, back when an airport kid could wander freely as pilots swaggered past. I'd just ducked beneath a Twin Beech when I saw her parked at the end of the row. She hadn't been there yesterday and judging from the long-dried bugs on her wings, she flew a lot and would be gone tomorrow—the sort of love you don't need but can't resist.

Her fuselage was slender, her cowling round and full of the promise of horsepower. A thin trickle of oil dripped into a crust of

9

snow below. It fell the way a drop of red wine might run down a woman's chin if she laughed at something you'd said over dinner. Uninvited, I wiped at the oil and then paused to stare up at her narrow windshield, beneath which was her name in flowing cursive—Betty Bounce. I said it aloud to feel it on my lips—Betty Bounce....

Her strutless wings invited me to look inside. Slowly I put my hand to the glass and peered at her dark instrument panel where strange dials and knobs told me she had class. The black radios and an artificial horizon cocked to one side bespoke of a spirit born to travel. Betty could never stay in one place—she'd invite you along, but if you hesitated, she'd laugh and depart.

Overwhelmed with passion, I did what no respectable airport kid dared do—I opened her door and eased my face deep inside. The intoxicating smell of avgas, oil, and cracked leather rushed through my sinuses and drilled deep into that part of my brain where love flares for a moment and never quite dies.

Quickly, I shut the door. I'd gone too far so I ran off—knees weak, heart pounding with lust for this goddess of flight. Reaching the fence, I turned and she laughed ever so gently. We both knew I was too young, and we parted.

Decades later as I opened the door to another Cessna 195 at the Watsonville, California fly-in, the aroma of oil and avgas with a hint of cracked leather rushed over me. I looked up and smiled, because Betty was back. She wouldn't stay, of course, but at least we had time to reminisce.

© 2002

Chapter 2
Romance In The Air

"First Date"

Stephen was nervous. He'd admired her from across the ramp for two years but only recently found the courage to make his move. After a stuttering phone call, money changed hands, papers were signed, and she was his. Or as much his as any human might believe a biplane could be possessed. Still, he wanted to make a good first impression.

"Hello," was all he could manage while approaching her outside the hangar. She smiled cautiously back at him with sunlight flashing off her spinner. "I've read your book," he added and waved the owner's manual as proof of his worth.

"Oh, that," she answered, indicating she didn't think it her best feature. "You shouldn't believe everything they write about me."

"You sure have a big useful load," he said and instantly corrected, "I mean, for an old Marquart Charger."

"Old?" she snapped. "Makes me sound like some antique. I'm barely 25." Then paused. "Okay, 30…ish."

They both couldn't help grinning as he walked around her running his fingertips along her lower wing. "Not much dihedral," he noted, and she said, "You want stability, you should've found yourself a Cherokee."

That hurt, but he had it coming. "Sorry," he mumbled and absently plucked at a flying wire. She seemed to like it, responding with a soft bass note. He stared at her, thrilling at the web of struts and wires between her sweptback wings. Her windshield was cut low with the front cockpit covered, giving her a racy look that set his heart pounding.

"Well?" she purred. "You gonna preflight all day or fly?" She lowered her voice, "You do know how to fly, don't you, Steve?"

His voice cracked, "Sure." And without further invitation he grabbed an upper wing handle and, placing a foot on her lower wing, heard her complain, "Excuse me!"

"What?"

"Where it says, NO STEP, I really mean it. Please…"

He quickly moved his foot onto the walkway—"Sorry"—and swung the other leg over the cockpit rim as though he'd done this his whole life. In truth, he'd never flown open-cockpit but, as any young man might, he'd dreamt of this moment since building his first model biplane. The one he'd blown up with a cherry bomb.

"Comfortable?" she asked as he melted into the seat.

His sweaty left hand gently caressed the throttle. "Very." His feet tapped her rudder pedals. Strapped in, he peered around her elegant nose and shouted: "Clear!" His barbaric yawp told the world that he was about to claim his rightful place in the sky. Only, as with many first encounters, reality punctured fantasy.

"Rudder!" she screamed as they sped down the runway while swerving from edge to edge. After liftoff the flight became a blur of uncoordinated wingovers, shadows across the beach and a landing that can best be described as forgivable. But forgive she did, and years later, whenever they're flying together, Stephen grins and wonders what there ever was to be nervous about on that first date.

© 2011

"Aeromantics"

The morning fog withdrew, exposing the airport to intense sunlight beneath a Hollywood blue sky. To Brandon, a hopeless dreamer, it looked as though an art director had ordered it. And, then, on cue, an orange Champ taxied from the T-hangars headed for the runway. Brandon climbed into the fuel truck and double-clutched it into gear as he watched a Luscombe followed by a Swift taxi out, tails swinging in provocative s-turns. The pilots checked mags on the roll to save time getting airborne.

Envy gripped Brandon watching the little airplanes climb toward the shoreline to dust the tips off the fog bank. He'd never flown. Wanted to, but despite working at the airport for the past two years no one had offered, "Wanna fly?" Then, again, he'd never asked. It was simply beyond his dreams.

Brandon drove the fuel truck a short distance, stopping before a green Bonanza that had arrived earlier on the localizer. The owner was a tall man in loud plaid slacks who'd looked extremely pleased with himself as he barked the fuel order: "Hey, kid, top 'er off and get the windshield. Where's the courtesy car?"

Brandon didn't feel so bad later when he slopped avgas over the Bonanza's wing. A rag caught some, while the rest washed to the ramp. As usual, he'd been dreaming about what it might be like to fly a Cub along the beach, dodging pelicans and waving to fishing boats beyond the pier. And it was then he realized he wasn't alone.

"Any chance I can get some gas?" Her voice, pleasant but shy, grabbed him before Brandon could turn around. Even though she was new to the field, he'd seen her before—had stared at her, actually, although never this close up. Behind her stood a J-3 Cub, as blue as the sky and trimmed in yellow gleaned from the sun.

"Uhhh," was all he managed, and she stared at him, her face crinkling into a smile as he stammered, "I didn't see you taxi up."

"You looked so absorbed in your work." She indicated the avgas dripping off the Bonanza's trailing edge. "Good thing you don't smoke," she added and immediately thought, 'Gawd, that sounded dumb…'

"Yeah. Ka-Boom!" He laughed and thought, 'I sound like an idiot…'

By the time he'd repositioned the truck before her airplane and watched her undo the gas cap, Brandon knew he was in love. Passing the fuel hose to her, their hands brushed, and she quickly turned and stared into the tank to keep from looking back at him. Maybe it was the fumes or the sun on her head, but by the time she'd overfilled the tank, and he reached past her to mop it up, she knew she was in love. Only there was no way for one to tell the other until she blurted out: "Wanna fly?"

And forty years later, together, they still smile at the possibilities of avgas under a blue sky on bright Cub mornings.

© 2011

"Hangar Day"

Rain on the hangar's roof and the occasional crump of thunder emphasized what a poor day it was for flying. Kathleen lay face up on a creeper pushing herself across the floor in a lazy backstroke made by wiping her Bonanza's belly with a shop rag. She dragged beside her a brownie pan of solvent, and every few feet she'd dip the rag, wring and then rest her arm before reaching up to clean away a year of grime. Each spring she'd wait for the perfect hangar day to open the airplane for the I.A. mechanic who would arrive with mirrors and lights to gaze into dark places for trouble, signs of advanced age in a graceful machine that refused to respect time.

"It's over fifty," the mechanic would say.

"So am I," Kathleen would counter.

The mechanic would then point at the missing clips in the Goodyear brakes. "They don't even make those anymore."

And Kathleen would nod, look concerned, and pray that the old airplane doc could coax her love through for one more year, as they'd been doing together since she'd bought the Bonanza back when avgas was sixty cents a gallon, and Flight Service was located on the airport and used eyeballs and not computers to see the sky, and Kathleen's husband had shaken his head when she showed him the airplane with the For Sale sign and plastic flags hanging on the propeller. "An airplane? What're you gonna do with that?"

"Learn to fly."

"What're you nuts…?" And there was more about a mortgage and something about responsibility and her need to grow up, but by then she'd chosen. And, now, she crept along her Bonanza's underside caressing it clean. She ran her fingertips over the rivets and reaching the V-tail, she sat up to gaze at the broad expanse of fuselage to where it mated with the slender wings and its massive flaps. She could feel the sensation of entering the traffic pattern with gear and flaps up and then smoothly pulling back on the yoke while in a bank, and as the airspeed lowered, she'd flick the piano-key gear switch to drop the wheels, and she'd roll the other way and descend onto base leg while lowering the flaps with an almost identical piano-key switch and never confusing the two. Just staring at the airframe she could relive the thousands of approaches she'd made since the day she'd abandoned mortgages and adult perceptions of responsibility in favor of life.

"Looks as though you've got a head start on me," a gray-haired man called as he passed through the hangar's side door, shaking rain from his cap and setting a toolbox on the floor. "Already got the inspection plates off — good."

Kathleen smiled at the someone who decades before had asked, "What're you nuts?" and after she'd learned to fly, decided that he'd best be nuts, too, because spending a rainy day together inside a hangar is the next best thing to…well, you decide.

© 2006

"Never Better"

A woman never looks better than when she is at an airport. Airport guys not so much, dressed in oil-stained jeans, mismatched socks and faded EAA caps. It's truly amazing that airport guys have ever attracted women; miraculous the species hadn't died out long ago.

I'd been a lifelong airport guy when I met her—not at an airport but, instead, at a barbecue in the sand hills near the mouth of the Salinas Valley. No one there showed any interest in aviation leaving me to spend the afternoon sky gazing and talking to a skinny dog. The dog wasn't a pilot so we shared little except an appreciation for free barbecue. This relationship exposed two things: Feeding chicken bones to dogs is a bad idea. And the dog belonged to a cute woman who'd been seriously ignoring me. That changed when her dog suddenly made a hacking noise like a Continental O-470 cranking on a cold morning.

"Did you give a chicken bone to my dog?" I was surprised that a vicious accusation could emanate from such an adorable face.

"No..." I stammered in what was obviously a lie while hiding a plate the gagging mutt had licked clean.

Despite there being no graceful way to perform the Heimlich maneuver on a choking animal she managed to clear its airway so the dog could resume begging for scraps. The woman then turned away until five words prompted a backward glance. "Have you ever been flying?" I called and then added with expanding lameness: "I'm a flight instructor."

Her brown eyes narrowed into what I mistook for possible romance above the clouds. And the way her head tilted right as her torso shifted ever so gently left indicated I'd made contact. Her response — "Some" — lacked the enthusiasm I'd hoped for, but I interpreted it as an opening nonetheless. After explaining where I worked I extended an invitation to fly. Her bemused smile while turning away, though, portended doom.

Weeks later I lay stretched beneath a Super Cub's belly scrubbing exhaust stains when a King Air thrust-reversed to a howling stop on the runway and taxied toward the hangars. Burnt kerosene intensified the turbine intrusion, and I rolled from beneath the fuselage to glower with piston-flyer disdain.

Windshield glare masked the lone figure inside the cockpit. Then, barely had the props stopped when the air stairs dropped and out jumped the dog I'd almost killed at the barbecue. On its heels was…the woman I'd invited to fly.

She stepped from her King Air, paused to shut the door and then walked toward my Cub with her brown eyes admiring it and not me. As she reached the wingtip the dog was sniffing my face with rekindled barbecue lust.

"So, you fly," I mumbled as she ran her fingers along the Cub's struts. "Some." She smiled and asked, "Need any help?" But before I could answer she dipped a rag into the solvent pan, and no woman could ever have looked better.

© 2013

"Celluloid Pilot"

Jerry loved airplanes, movies and Louise, the cute flight instructor on the field. Sadly, she didn't know that the pilot, with thin sandy hair above a Jimmy Stewart face, existed. And Jerry was too shy to attempt more than a smile toward the woman he adored. Like Stewart, though, Jerry knew he looked good in the Starduster biplane he'd spent six years building and had yet to fly. And knowing how in movies the sky guy ultimately gets the girl….

"Face it," he sighed as she taxied past his hangar, "I don't stand a chance."

He turned toward his biplane, the true love that would always be loyal to its creator. Running his hand along its curvaceous red skin above the delicate tail feathers he was overwhelmed by the passion that had driven him to finish the airplane. Music from Those Magnificent Men in Their Flying Machines played in his head, and he decided that, today, he would fly the machine. Unfortunately, like many homebuilders, he hadn't flown much since beginning the project.

"I know this airplane," he rationalized aloud. "I built every part. Where the rigging was a little tight, I've tuned the flying wires to perfection." He plucked one, and it sounded a cello bass note.

Humming a Prussian march, he pushed the little biplane from its hangar. The woman who ran the fuel truck drove by, smiled and waved.

"Morning, Madam," Jerry called and blushed at his sudden courage. He donned a leather flying helmet, placed his foot on the wing and hesitated. It'd been six years since he'd flown, except for a quick BFR from an instructor more interested in cash than instructing.

Inside the open cockpit, he looked for Louise. He wanted her to see his Errol Flynn Dawn Patrol élan with sunlight flashing off his goggles. Instead, she was washing her Cherokee, oblivious to his internal screenplay. It was a warm day, and her legs were bare beneath un-CFI-like shorts. She rubbed a sudsy sponge in "Cool Hand Luke" swirls across the windshield. He'd planned to go once around the pattern, but, now, he must be the cinematic barnstormer, Waldo Pepper, wowing the crowd to win the girl.

At the runway's end he opened the throttle. The nose pulled left. Tires squeaked. He considered aborting, but for her eyes only he pushed the joystick forward to lift the tail and swerved further off the centerline. Had he pulled back, the biplane might've flown, and he'd be the star in his fast-forward mind movie. Instead, he stomped right rudder and sliced across a runway light. The propeller spit glass shards like flak, and six years of work ground-looped in the weeds.

First to reach the site was Louise. Seeing him climb unhurt from the wreckage, she sniffed back a tear and laughed, "Statistically, flying is still the safest form of transportation." Upon hearing her quote Superman, the Bogart in Jerry replied, "I think this is the start of a beautiful friendship."

Music up. Fade to black?

©2009

"Love Flies Out"

Joe faced his biplane unable to speak. The 1928 Travel Air 4000 didn't seem willing to listen, making this the most awkward moment in their relationship. "All those years," the biplane hissed, but Joe could only shrug, meaning, "These things happen..." And he turned to push the hangar door fully open.

That was a mistake. The morning sunlight wrapped the old biplane in a Hollywood embrace. Her deep burgundy skin glowed as though sucking energy from the sun's core. Vengeful silver needles flashed off her flying wires, piercing Joe's eyes as he looked back in shame at what he secretly still loved. "These aren't tears," he protested and wiped a sleeve across his face. He reached to touch the lower wing, but the airplane recoiled, implying that she'd been betrayed.

She was considerably older than Joe, but they'd agreed this wouldn't be an issue. "Flight is ageless," they'd said to each other that day Joe saw her on the ramp with the For Sale sign on her prop. "We'll ignore reality and fly as though we were both born yesterday." Thus, vows exchanged, they did fly. From seacoast to inland valleys, across hot prairies in summer and frosted ridgelines in early winter. Joe smiled recalling the morning they'd inscribed parallel tread marks on fresh snow across a frozen mountain lake. She smiled remembering it, too. And, then, she laughed reminding him of the time they'd landed on wet grass after a thunderstorm. Joe picked up the story, saying it wasn't his fault they'd ground looped. "The wind was stronger than it looked," he defended himself.

"You didn't know my rudder yet," she shot back and paused. She couldn't stay mad at him. Her voice softened, "Those were good times." Joe nodded and suddenly felt he couldn't go through with it. But the moment was interrupted when a Beech Baron taxied toward the hangar. The propellers had barely stopped turning before a young man climbed out, jumped from the wing and ran toward them.

"Sorry I'm late," he called. His dark hair, pulled back in ponytail, bounced against his leather flight jacket collar. He took Joe's proffered hand but stared past him at the Travel Air. "She's beautiful," he stammered. Joe released his grip and watched the young man move slowly around the biplane's nose. "More beautiful than you'd let on." And it was obvious the young man was in love. Obvious, too, the Travel Air was about to forget all about Joe.

It was easier that way once Joe realized what a shameless hussy his old flame could be. She'd found another lover, and, later, as Joe stood clutching a cashier's check, he watched his longtime love fly away. At the controls was a smiling young pilot, unaware that one day this timeless goddess of flight would break his heart, too.

That night, alone in the empty hangar, Joe ran his finger down a column of classified ads. One teased: "Waco, Taperwing, 1929, Make Offer…" And love flew in again.

Chapter 3
Fantasy Flight

"Ailerona"

There's a place in the Midwest approachable only from the sky. It's south of Canada and a bit north of Mexico. Draw a line along the eastern edge of the Rockies, and it's to the right of that and west of Youngstown, Ohio, maybe Columbus. It's strictly a middle-of-America place, although there have been reports of it north of International Falls, and it was once spotted in California's Central Valley, and along the Snake River in Idaho, although I suspect those were false sightings. No one's seen it in New Jersey since 1966.

This place is called Ailerona. It has no ICAO identifier, doesn't appear on any sectional or airport guide. It can't be loaded into a GPS database; if you tried, you'd blow the RAIM guts out of the box.

Despite the lack of navaids, Ailerona is supposedly easy to find if you know how to look. I haven't been there myself, but I once met a pilot in Wagner, South Dakota who knew a guy in Alliance, Nebraska, who'd flown over Ailerona one winter day in a Maule. He said it appeared through a crystalline veil of snow and looked like sunrise at noon. He reported an expanse of green across low hills above which a Super Cub flew in loose formation with a Taperwing Waco until the Cub descended to an upsloping pasture where the cows turned their heads to marvel at the appropriateness of a Cub in their salad bar.

Ailerona appeared briefly in Greek mythology when Icarus tried to fly across the Mediterranean in his waxwing homebuilt in search of this perfect place. He looked too hard however, and his wings melted. Ever since the FAA has denied Ailerona's existence fearing that if pilots saw its wooden hangars full of Stearmans, Fairchilds, and Lockheed Vegas and Lodestars, if they saw the fuel truck hauling both 100 and 80-octane at 35 and 30 cents respectively, if pilots saw all that, they'd question the way things are.

I thought I saw Ailerona up in Michigan while standing beneath a Husky's wing during a thunderstorm that looked like creation itself. Another time, it flashed briefly through my old Bonanza while scud running between a low overcast and the flat pine forests of northern Minnesota. I skimmed the trees at 150 knots through a 300-foot wedge of clear air that led nowhere and I hoped would never end. But each time that I thought I saw Ailerona it disappeared. I tried to grasp it, to log the moment for spiritual currency and, in the process; the vision said I wasn't ready and faded away.

Ailerona holds the raw stuff of flight from biplanes to the Concorde. It's where aviation began and, today, is the one corner of flight where no one can clip your wings. It's out there, and chances are you've already seen it—perhaps in that perfect instrument approach or the beautifully executed crosswind landing. It may even exist outside the Midwest, although what better place to begin the search?

© 1981

"Wash Me"

Luke's Cessna 140 sat alone in the end hangar near the wash area, waiting. The day had been miserably hot. Incessant desert winds rattled the tin roof, making the dripping hose look so inviting through the crack in the door. It'd been weeks since Luke had taken her flying, weeks of heat and dust inside the metal box. Wasps stopped filling her air vents, because it'd become so hot. But the wind had shifted that afternoon, and with it the sound of Luke's motorcycle squeaking to a stop outside the hangar brought hope.

A lock snapped, and the hangar door slid open. Without so much as a "Sorry I haven't paid attention to you lately" Luke grabbed the Cessna by the propeller and pulled. She could tell he'd been on the ground too long and wanted to fly. But for an instant the C-140 considered making her mags hot to slap away his sweaty hand. "Just who do you think you are coming out here like this, assuming I'd be willing to go up with you?"

Instead, she locked her brakes. Luke glanced down at the wheels where he expected to see chocks in place. Nothing. Taking the prop in both hands he tugged again, and, again, the old two-seater dug in her treads. "I will not be seen on the runway like this!"

Luke sighed. He'd had a rough week. It was hot, and he just wanted to fly. But seeing the dusty airplane, her windshield nearly opaque from neglect, he relented. And as soon as she sensed this, the 140 released her brakes and allowed him to pull her toward the wash rack.

The water was hot from sitting in the coiled hose in the sun. But as it was replaced with cold they both smiled, admitting how good it felt. Luke found an old towel, and, soaking down the airplane he'd

23

known since high school, he moved around her, flushing her with cold water and wiping away the grit. He'd named her Lucille and had painted her name in red script across the engine cowling. The letters glistened beneath the water droplets. He wiped her clean and enjoyed the cold wet flushing his sneakers. Then, slipping beneath her belly, he lay on his back to scrub away the oily grime, transferring it to his own clothes. When he stood to wipe the tail Luke was soaked, filthy and happy. Running a cool hand along her fuselage he remembered how good they were together, and he reached for her door.

Locked.

He tugged. The sun slipped below the hills. Soon the fog would roll in from the bay, killing any chance to fly this gorgeous airplane. "Come on," he pleaded. But catching his reflection in her polished aluminum skin, he saw what she saw—a grubby pilot in wet, greasy jeans and t-shirt.

"You're not planning to take me up like that, are you?" she asked what wasn't a question. And Luke knew he'd never fully understand airplanes.

© 2010

"We Gotta Talk"

Roy slid the hangar door shut on his Cirrus. When it hit the stop with a kettledrum Bong, he thought he'd caught someone's foot: "Hey, you!"

He turned but saw no one. "Yah, I'm talking to you, Roy," and Roy answered, "Who's calling?"

"You know darn well who's addressing you, mister," and Roy peeked through the crack between the door halves. "Yah, sure. Now, open up on account of we gotta talk." The voice sounded not only annoyed but also disturbingly Scandinavian. Roy slid the door wide enough to step inside and saw his airplane parked just where he'd left it minutes before—time he'd planned to spend on the freeway headed toward important stuff.

"Such as?" the Cirrus asked.

"S…such as what?" Roy slowly answered having never spoken to an airplane before.

"You're thinkin' about doing something more important than flying. What could that possibly be?"

"How do you...? I, I have an appointment."

"If you called it a 'rendezvous' you'd sound more interesting. You're not very interesting, Roy."

"It's work, it's not meant to be interesting, just important. I have to go."

"Phhhhttttppp!"

Roy dropped his briefcase and approached the wing. Staring into the windshield he addressed his own smirking reflection and accused, "Did you just blow a razzberry at me?"

"That was for the landing."

"What was wrong with my landing?"

"What was right with it? It hurt. You stink, mister. You don't use my rudders, you don't roll aileron into the wind. In short, you expect me to do all the work. "

"Oh, I don't have to take this," and Roy reached for his briefcase. "I own you!"

"Phhhhttttppp!"

"I'm not listening."

"How long you plan to leave them bugs on me, eh?"

"You're going in for an oil change on the twenty-third, I'll tell them to wash you then."

"You gonna tell them to fly me as well?"

"No, I do the flying."

"You ride, you never fly. You haven't changed since we left Duluth..."

"I rescued you from Duluth, buster."

"Okay, one for you. But now it's time you learned who I am."

"Who you are? You're an airplane, my airplane; I paid for you and fly you just the way the owner's manual says to. I upgrade your GPS database when it's time and comply with all the service bulletins..."

"Ever flown at sunset?"

"Sure, I've flown at official sunset, and an hour after dark, too. Three landings to a full stop every...."

"I mean at the sunset, nose pointed into the crimson ball on the horizon like you'd fly straight into the fire and we'd melt..."

"Oh, you're nuts."

"Yah, I'm nuts. Who's the one talkin' to his airplane?" And before Roy could respond, the Cirrus barely suppressed a yawn with, "Be quiet shutting the hangar door. The Cherokee next store has been complaining." And Roy stared at what he thought was his airplane and said, "You won't tell anyone about this, will ya?"

"Not as long as we keep talkin'."

©2006

"Will Fly 4...."

Jack flipped the light switches—one killed the interior light, and the other lit the rotating beacon atop the FBO shack. He stepped backwards through the door—and time—locking both behind him. "What a day." His voice was hoarse from repeating: "More aileron...opposite rudder...nose up...."

Spent radio chatter echoed inside his brain, including the ridiculous phrase, "Traffic in the area, please advise." He wanted to turn it all off, go home and forget flight instructing for the night. And that's when a shadow in the green beacon flash brushed past him.

"Ah, can I help you?" Jack asked.

"You're the one in need of help," the stranger quipped and opened the door to flip on the lights. Stepping inside he added, "C'mon, day's not over yet." He turned to Jack who noticed that they were the same height with the same hair—thin brown going gray. The stranger's voice was familiar and said, "Yeah, I'm you. And before you say 'Me?' in Rod Serling disbelief, just think about it."

Jack tried, but having flown every day since Memorial Day, he could only stare at his own image, which said, "You're literally passing yourself coming and going."

"I have been flying a lot."

"Like I don't know that?"

"Well, it's summer. You'd think that gas prices would've killed business, but everyone wants to fly..."

"A pox upon them for overworking the poor instructor—boo-hoo-hoo."

"Are you making fun of me?"

"Yes." Jack recoiled from his tormenting self as it asked, "Who was your first student this morning?"

26

Jack thought. "That was twelve hours ago, maybe, fourteen. In between I've flown with ... was her name, um, Allison?"

"Correct, sir," and his other self hit the service bell on the counter—Ding! "Now, for a week's CFI's wages—"

"Such a small wager."

"Can you tell me what—if anything—she learned from you?"

Jack was too tired to think and slumped onto the couch. "I don't know. Was she the instrument student?"

"Oh, Jackie boy, you're exhausted, no good to anyone. Might as well have a laptop in the right seat acting as the instructor."

"Hey, we're not Part 141!"

"You get some sleep, and I'll take over for the night." The apparition said and walked outside toward the flight line. Jack couldn't protest and momentarily closed his eyes only to reawake in what seemed to be seconds.

"Excuse me," a polite voice tapped his brain back to life.

"Huh?" Jack mumbled and squinted into flaming sunlight. "Who are you?" he asked an angelic silhouette.

"Allison. I'm scheduled for my first flying lesson. The door was open and...I could come back some other time."

"First lesson?" Jack pushed himself upright, yawned and looked around. "Was there another instructor here? Looks kinda like me?" The new student backed away saying, "Maybe, I should just go—"

"No," Jack objected and looked into a slightly anxious face of another earthling ready to fly. That almost renewed his energy, so he asked, "Got any money?"

© 2008

"Please Advise"

Sunrise flooded the subdivisions, malls and freeway below as Fred broke from the clouds. "Cancel IFR," he radioed through a yawn. The approach controller, having been awake all night, mumbled, "Squawk VFR..."

Fred changed frequencies and announced: "Four-point-seven northwest. Traffic in the area, please advise." Tired as he was he marveled at his GPS precision, so it was jarring when a woman answered, "Advise what?"

"Ah, advise your position." But she replied, "Look outside now and then and you'd know."

Fred scanned for the traffic that refused to identify itself. "That's not funny!"

"Wasn't meant to be." Then after a short pause she asked, "Where's your shadow?"

"My what?"

"Shadow. Everybody's got one, like bellybuttons. Where's yours?"

Fred ignored the voice and returned to the glass instrument panel. "You won't find it there," she laughed. Fred was about to tell her to shut up when the panel vanished, replaced by a few round instruments. He then realized that his left hand that had grasped the multi-function control stick, now held a throttle knob. His right held a joystick poking through dusty floorboards, vibrating with unfamiliar engine noises that competed with the surrounding wind. And everything smelled of scorched oil and something sweet he couldn't identify.

"Dope and fabric," the voice said. "Only toy airplanes are made of plastic." Fred saw that he was no longer inside a computerized flying machine. Instead, he flew something with massive wings both above and below him. Where seconds before there'd been a smooth cowl housing an unseen engine, now black cylinders spit oil back at the windshield.

Terrified, he glanced above at cloud bottoms and then slowly to his left where his chin nearly touched an open cockpit's rim. Peering over it he saw orchards and strawberries fields stretching to the foothills where he knew factories and houses should be. The freeway had shriveled to a narrow ribbon with a few square cars moving slowly along. And ahead was a stretch of dirt runway beside wooden hangars. "I advise," she warned, "that you fly the airplane."

One pilot's heaven is another's hellish nightmare. Fred blinked, unsure if he'd been asleep or was still so. He wanted to climb from his seat and shout, "I'm not playing this game!" But he had no choice and had to fly the biplane.

Nothing on the panel helped. No GPS marked his progress or worth. Only her soft voice coaching: "Reduce power...ease back on the stick—not so abruptly!" And the biplane's shadow caught the tailskid as Fred smacked the dirt in a less-than-pretty landing.

No sooner had the biplane stopped than a 1929 Model A postal truck pulled alongside. "Morning, Freddie," the driver called as she stuffed mail sacks into the biplane's cargo hold. "You look awful. Getting enough sleep?" Fred shrugged, and the driver smiled. "All loaded. If there's anything else you need, please advise."

And the strange vision Fred had dreamed of some futuristic world where pilots couldn't fly without asking for advice mercifully faded.

© 2012

"A Hole In The Sky"

It took weeks for anyone to notice, because so few people looked up any more. They're too busy staring at little screens in their palms. But one day someone noticed that a hole had appeared in the sky just above the Santa Cruz Mountains. Immediately, news anchors and scientists competed to explain the gap in space. Senate commissions formed, and the president tried to reassure an anxious world that the missing bit of firmament—the shape of a barn door—warranted no need for panic.

Therefore, most people did. Accusations flew. Banks failed. Hordes stocked up on bottled water, batteries and DVDs. FEMA launched four aerial balloons with each trailing a steel cable to hoist an immense curtain over the hole, but without pilots they soon drifted away leaving the image exposed.

Crowds gathered on the beach at sunset to stare at the gap where stars once shone. Through a small telescope you could see a vague female form, and if you stared long enough you'd swear she'd waved. So many waved back. And giggled.

Some worshipped the vision, while others grew to loathe it and swore vengeance against whoever was responsible. But the vast majority, especially those who'd never actually seen it, felt mildly afraid and complained that someone should do something about it. This proved fine with those in charge who couldn't explain the hole but wanted to retain control of it.

Del Critty knew better. Being the last aviator on the planet he ignored the hysteria as he drove the last Corvair—a 1965—to the last airport, slipped past TSA and entered his hangar. Inside, coated in memory dust and sparrow musings, was the last small airplane on earth, a homebuilt Pietenpol Air Camper. Del hadn't flown since manned flight had been outlawed, and swore he'd never visit the airport again. But when he saw the sky peek open and faced the image, he knew someone was calling, and he couldn't ignore her any longer.

It was late afternoon when he pushed the parasol-winged two-seater from the hangar and struggled to climb alone into the open cockpit. He wondered if he would remember how to fly but felt Claire's presence guiding his hands and feet over the controls. His eyes stung as he scanned the walnut instrument panel that they'd spent so many weeks designing together.

Despite neglect the airplane's engine popped to life. Del reached around the windshield to smear away dust with his handkerchief and then released it into the slipstream. It'd been so long since any airplane had departed the condemned airfield that few recognized the sound. Still, thousands cheered upon seeing the Pietenpol climbing above the hills and directly toward the hole in the sky. Eyeballs to the many telescopes watched the airplane fly through that door as Claire, once again seated in the front cockpit, turned to smile at Del. Then, as the door closed, and the cheering faded, the crowds returned to staring at the little screens in their palms.

© 2011

Chapter 4
Learning To Fly

"An Executive Decision"

Her voice over the phone was polite and to the point, someone who was comfortable solving problems through logical research and smooth implementation of a well-reasoned plan. I knew this couldn't be one of my pilot friends. Her name was Susan, and her father, Vic, kept his Luscombe in the hangar behind mine. He'd occasionally take her for a ride, so her request sounded reasonable: "I want to learn to land an airplane, in case something happens."

She made it sound like enrolling in CPR class; this was a skill to be acquired but never used. She explained that she had no interest in learning to fly, only how to return safely to Earth—should something happen. We agreed on a three-lesson package in my Aeronca Champ—so many dollars for just enough skill to survive and nothing more.

Tuesday afternoon we met at the hangar where I walked her through a preflight with the basic what-makes-what-do-what-and-why-there's-no-radio. She took notes on a legal pad while I wiped oil on my pants when I couldn't find a rag. She knew that old airplanes don't start with keys so wasn't shocked when I spun the propeller by hand. She set the throttle where I said to and pushed the rudders precisely as instructed to taxi. It was a cool day, and the airplane performed beautifully. Another flight instructor might say that was caused by denser air, but I suspected it was the result of an airplane trying to impress a nonbeliever.

We practiced turns and then slowed until the cockpit was almost quiet with a cold wind slipping through the open window. She briefly stuck her hand outside to feel the sky, and as we descended she looked where our shadow drifted across barren trees and fields. Following the two-lane highway that snakes up from Missouri, she no doubt also saw the deer as they came out of the woods to feed. I pointed to a hawk, but she'd already spotted it and watched it slide beneath our wing giving us a tolerant nod in passing.

On landing, Susan stretched to look past the airplane's nose as the tail settled onto the dead grass. Back at the hangar she opened her day planner and asked, "How's Thursday and Friday look for you?" I've always liked Thursdays and Fridays, so I agreed to meet again, and she left.

By the end of the third and final lesson on Friday Susan made more-than-survivable landings and had fulfilled her goal to be able to land should something happen to her father. She was safe, and I'd earned my fee. But as the sunlight faded to the afterglow of flight, something happened to Susan. It happens to all those who approach flight thinking it possible to convince an airplane that your plans really matter.

"I want to learn to fly," she said in a voice more confident than the one that had requested simply to learn to land. Something, indeed, had happened, but, now, all the goals had changed.

©2002

"Dreamstormin"

Chances are you've seen them staring at clouds. Sometimes they just sit inside hangars and do nothing as though listening to airplanes talk. They're more than daydreamers. They're dreamstormers, renegades from the other side of the sky where flight doesn't arrive at Gate 21B. These misfits believe that the sky is an amphitheater open to anyone who might look its way. Unashamed, they lure others to gaze upward and be caught in an infinite net of wind and adventure.

When forced back to Earth these sky people seem to retain traces of clouds inside their heads. Perhaps, that's how they cope with the gravity-stricken world. They rarely have any money, and what they glean inevitably slips into the cockpit. Some of these dreamers have managed to hold jobs, working undetected beside wide-awake humans. Clever dreamers may appear to be alert and nod politely when the non-dreamers try to rally them with corporate cries to Go Forward! In truth, these pilots are dreaming of dew running off fabric-covered biplane wings. Or they're flying a Luscombe at sunset over a soft Monterey Bay fogbank. Maybe the dreamer who appears to be listening to a presidential debate is actually re-flying her first solo in a Cessna 150. Thirty years later she can still reach for the flaps in her sleep. Wouldn't it be great if political candidates could dream of wings instead of merely promising us dreams? Perhaps, there'd be fewer nightmares. But I dream.

Dreamstormers live outwardly stable lives. They mow lawns, floss daily and even raise families. To non-flyers they may appear normal, but as we dreamers catch our reflections in a Bonanza's polished spinner, we see the smile. We know that while the rest of the world thinks it's awake, it actually sleeps—unaware that dreams can storm into an open mind and take over.

I'd just paid for fuel and turned as a man walked through the FBO's entrance from the parking lot. He looked confused, and I assumed from his brown uniform shirt and matching pants that he was delivering something. "Can I help you?" Dan asked, and the deliveryman answered, "No." Then, he shuddered as though trying to shake himself awake and looked through the glass at the rental Cessna on the ramp. "Can I..." he started to ask. "How..." he struggled for the words, unaware that he was dreamstorming and couldn't make non-flyer words express his desire.

"Fly?" Dan prompted with an accompanying hand gesture as though addressing an alien. And the alien grunted a yes. Through the glass I saw a brown delivery truck idling in the parking lot. The front left wheel was over the curb and on the grass. It was apparent this dormant soul had left for his deliveries, thinking he was wide-awake. But when passing the airport, he must've seen an airplane glide low across the highway, and he began to dream. Only to discover what we dreamers know: All dreams lead to the airport, where the real awakening begins.

© 2008

"A Good Day To Fly"

James stared at the calendar above the workbench where a dead Franklin engine awaited someone to claim the TBO'd remains. He hated giving customers bad news: "We did everything we could ..." But they'd sob and pointlessly beg for him to check again. "No," he'd insist, "It's time. I'm sorry." James wasn't really all that sorry, because shop work made up for some of what he lost on his lone rental—a tired Cessna 150.

He'd rebuilt the two-seater so many times James couldn't tell which parts were original. Still, the forty-something trainer continued to suffer student landings as though it'd just left the Kansas factory. And, perhaps its long service caused James to reflect on the calendar's date—May 14.

We like to think that we'll always remember where they were on a particular date, such as when JFK died. James, however, couldn't recall. "I was nine," he'd admit. "What'd I know?" He couldn't remember because on that 1963 November day he was staring out the classroom window at airplanes flying close enough to steal his soul away. Pilots are easily distracted, but as he considered the calendar he knew exactly where he was on May 14, 1974 when he was a student pilot in Hawaii.

"Take 'er around the pattern," his instructor, David Ho, had said to him after signing his logbook. "If you survive, I'll wave you on for two more laps." And just before David closed the door sealing James alone inside the new Cessna 150, he added, "And, please, this time try to land with the nose up. These things have to last a few years."

Ever since, James has felt disappointed that he can't remember the exact moment his wheels left the runway. He has no memory of soaring alone and touching whatever god's face supposedly hid among the clouds. Truth is, he can't recall much of his first solo pattern except that he landed as he always had with three bounces halfway down the runway. Taxiing back, he looked toward his instructor standing in the grass and interpreted his shaking head to indicate he should go again.

The third pattern he could recall, because by then he'd calmed down enough to look beyond the instrument panel toward the tropical sky. Clouds piled in marshmallows against the green hills beyond the pineapple fields. And far in his distant memory he could still see the sacred outline of Pearl Harbor and beyond that Honolulu's misty sprawl. And then he landed, and it was over. He'd soloed, and watching his instructor sign the shirttail James absorbed the date: May 14.

Now, as he turned away from the calendar to meet his student, Mary Ellen, he saw in her face the old airplane's future. "It's May 14th," James said as he climbed into the Cessna 150's right seat and added, "It's a good day to fly." And running his hand across the cracked plastic panel, he thought, "Still gotta get a few more years out these things."

© 2008

"Will Fly 4 Tomatoes"

Pull up to a light in your '67 Mustang, and some bald guy will stare with two glazed doughnuts for eyes. "I had one of those," he'll mutter to the decades gone. "In high school…" and memories of summer nights with a forgotten prom queen will carry him back. Old airplanes have that same power.

The rain had passed leaving an evening sky so clear I thought it might crack. I pushed the 1946 Aeronca from the hangar as an old farmer walked toward me. A seed cap shaded his face, but his eyes swept the airframe, peeling back time. "I learned in one those," he said more to the airplane than to me. He reached to touch it and hesitated. "Go ahead," I said, and he gently ran his calloused fingers along where the fuselage curves into the tail. The caress awakened something inside him and the machine. "You instruct?" he asked the way farmers do without asking what they really want to know. I nodded, yes, and skipped the next step of haggling price—you'll never win against a farmer. "Just going to warm up the oil before I change it," I said, even though I wasn't. "Hop in the front."

His boots dragged against the doorframe and left muddy clods on the varnished floorboards. He told me he hadn't flown in years, but he didn't need help to find the seatbelt. "We didn't have no headsets when I learned," he said. Still, he accepted the one I handed him but didn't listen as I explained how the intercom worked. "Instructor, back then, used to smack you upside the head to get you to center the ball." And before I could answer he added, "And everyone had to demonstrate a two-turn spin before you could solo." I didn't explain that many flight instructors, today, couldn't teach spins.

Ten minutes later he pointed through the open side window at his farmhouse below, white with a green roof. I could almost smell the nearby garden edged with tomato vines. Surrounding cornfields pulsed in the wind, tracing gusts in swirls of shifting green and yellow. Fat cattle ate their way through a pasture like restless Volkswagens. They grew smaller as we climbed. And they twirled like bugs in a blender after I closed the throttle, pulled up the nose and called, "You got it!" He kicked left rudder and with the stick full aft, spun the world back to 1946. After two turns he recovered and pulled up for another.

I admit I was dizzy by the time we landed. Time travel has that effect on me. When he offered to pay, I said his money was no good. But I when I mentioned his garden, he smiled and left. Later, after I shut the hangar, I walked to my truck where I found a paper bag full of the reddest fruit the sky can deliver. And the next day I taped a sign to my airplane's window: Will Fly 4 Tomatoes.

© 2007

"Soon"

"When do I solo?" Franklin asked. His face betrayed the anticipation and fear of rejection that student pilots can't hide. Jim, the instructor, wanted to say, "When you quit trying to kill us," but, instead, answered, "Soon."

He knew that meant nothing, like being told your pizza will be ready in 20 minutes or that your call is important to us. This student wouldn't solo until he learned how to land on the mains and not on the nose wheel. He also knew that Franklin had no feel for flying. Enthusiasm, perhaps, but he lacked the gut sense of how the machine transitions from soft sky to unyielding earth. Jim patiently repeated the steps to a successful landing, just as he'd done countless times before. The student nodded in return, but the hollow glow in his eyes told Jim that the feel for the airplane wasn't there–not yet.

Still, Franklin had money and drive, both of which instructors appreciate, so on they flew, grinding around the traffic pattern through the last of the summer afternoons. Occasionally, Franklin seemed to glimpse enlightenment, prompting Jim to cheer, "Yes, that's it, nose up...bring it up...hold it...keep the rudder in..." And the mains would skim against the pavement in a rubbery smooch. "Great, let's do another!" And up they'd go only to have Franklin make the next approach as though he'd suffered total amnesia on downwind. There was no crosswind correction, no flare, just another side-loaded, three-point flop against the runway. Undaunted, though, Franklin would ask: "When do I solo?"

"Soon," Jim sighed. "Soon..."

But then–as happens in all fairy tales–a cool breeze fluffed the windsock atop the hangar, and a miracle occurred. Franklin got it. Wasn't a darn thing Jim had said. He hadn't introduced any new teaching technique. Franklin simply felt how flight worked and made three smooth landings in a row.

"Quick, give me your logbook," Jim stammered before the magic could dissipate. Flipping to a back page he endorsed his student to leave the planet alone. "Do three laps around the pattern," he said. "Full stop, taxi back. Watch speed and coordination in the turns and remember a go-around is always an option." He rapped out the same benediction he'd given every student about to become something greater than the sum of all human mass on the planet.

Minutes later, Jim stood beside the runway in the lonely flight instructor pose trying to appear casual but silently terrified that he'd overlooked something. But he hadn't. Franklin was ready and proved it by making a smooth first landing, an acceptable second and a truly dorky but safe third landing.

Back inside the office, as Jim clipped his son's shirttail, he had to admit that as slow a learner as he was, Franklin had soloed in half the time it had taken him to learn. And that's when the future pilot asked, "When do I take my checkride?"

Jim considered all the work yet to come, and replied, "Soon."

© 2010

"Solo Bliss"

Flight instructors know when a student nears solo, because things go to hell. Recalling my own pre-solo, I remember much whimpering and flailing about the Cessna 150's cockpit. I was amazed how relieved the instructor seemed when he stumbled from the airplane muttering, "I can't take this." He signed my logbook and fled for an airline career.

On my third pass around the pattern, the control tower wisely quit trying to sequence me and simply cleared traffic from my path. Years later when I was a controller I understood why. Students occasionally haven't a clue what lies beyond their spinners. That was certainly as far as I could focus. I dutifully followed the pattern procedures: Set downwind power and trim. I then keyed the microphone to override whoever was speaking in order to announce my intentions. Tower, in turn, yelled at me, and I acknowledged with "Roger." This meant I didn't understand a word of what ATC had said, so I turned base leg where I always did, intercepting something large with two engines.

On final, with airspeed stabilized at red line, I added flaps and immediately climbed. I was impressed how much better the airplane performed without 200 pounds of instructor. More flaps didn't help, until I finally realized I needed to reduce power. Threats turned to pleading from the tower where a red light beamed at me. "Pretty," I thought, as I lowered the visor and aimed kamikaze-style at the runway.

I remember a big number 6 in the windshield and couldn't understand why the tower was sending other airplanes around on runway 24. I was busy watching that 6 vanish beneath my spinner. Had I looked back I would've seen it diminish behind the tail as well. But I couldn't turn around; I had to stare ahead and hope. Academically, I knew I was supposed to add aileron for the crosswind. Opposite rudder would've kept the nose pointed down the pavement, but I chose, instead, to do nothing and await divine intervention. Meanwhile, I congratulated myself for holding altitude so nicely ten feet above the runway. I knew that, with patience, Bernoulli and Newton would raise the planet to meet my wheels. Eventually, halfway down the runway, they did with a sound like a garbage can tossed from a speeding truck.

Decades later, I was seated beside a student who, like the younger me, held altitude nicely ten feet above the runway. I knew he was waiting for it all to come together. When it did, I stumbled from the forty-year-old Cessna 150. "I can't take this," I muttered. "Gimme your logbook." It was obvious that he was ready to solo. Then, I watched him in the pattern, wishing I could teach him just a little more. But I realized it had to be this way. The universe demanded payback for all the bad karma I'd created when beginning my quest for the nirvana of perfect flight. And with practice, I may reacquire that ideal student mind.

© 2007

"That Gentle Touch"

Kate limped slightly from long-ago motorcycle spills and didn't hear well after a lifetime spent around airplane engines. "If you'd just quit mumbling I'd hear fine," she'd growl if you mentioned a hearing aid. Any suggestion to ever see a doctor brought quick rebuke: "And have to tell the feds? What the FAA don't know won't hurt me."

She was slow climbing into her Pitts but once strapped in, her voice rang out: "Clear prop!" Locals took that more as a threat than a courtesy: "Move or you're chopped liver!"

Kate didn't waste words on the radio, either. "Biplane departing one-nine," was all she'd offer and felt that anyone who didn't get the gist was too stupid to fly. In short, Kate Strauss was a seasoned airport manager who could fly better than anyone with or without a legitimate pilot certificate. And no one dared ask to see hers.

Me? Not so seasoned. I'd just paid too much for a 1946 Aeronca Champ, skipped the pre-buy inspection and, most importantly, didn't know beans about flying tail wheel. Ignorance has never delayed me before, so I climbed into the airplane, remembered it didn't have an electrical system and stumbled back out to hand-prop it. I was impressed how quickly an unattended airplane taxis with no one at the controls. Diving into the cockpit and groping for the throttle, I made a note to chock the wheels next time. And that's when I noticed Kate's Pitts and waved to her as she hurriedly pulled off the taxiway and onto the grass allowing me to pass. She didn't wave back.

I spent the next hour in the pattern bouncing and swerving down the runway. I felt I was getting the hang of it and figured the cost of rapidly wearing tires into my learning expenses. Then, I spotted Kate's Pitts circling overhead. Like a hawk watching a mindless rodent below, she waited until I'd cleared the runway—via a short detour through the weeds—before descending. Unlike my landing, hers was smooth. She quickly taxied past me, stopped and signaled to pull over. I did.

She climbed onboard and sighed, "I can't stand it. Someone's gotta teach you how to land this poor thing." And before I could respond she demanded, "Show me your feet!" Baffled, I pointed at the rudder pedals. "Good," she said. "Now, let's attach them to your brain."

I'd like to remember that Kate turned into a soothing voice of patience once in the instructor's seat. Instead, she slapped me upside the head on every uncoordinated turn. "Rudder! Quit leaning! This ain't no bobsled!"

Motivated by shame I began flying, if not with finesse, at least without disaster. Later, after Kate crawled stiffly from the airplane, I asked, "Do you want to sign my logbook?" She merely shook her head and said, "What the FAA don't know won't hurt you." And off she limped to confront an unsuspecting Cherokee pilot who'd just porpoised to a stop on her runway.

"You See, Grasshopper"

It was one of the last days of autumn when the temperature was still well above freezing and the grass had turned from dull green to almost yellow. A breeze gently rocked the hangar door as it rode up and slid back on its tracks above the biplane's nose. Grasshoppers popped through the opening like airline passengers clearing security oblivious of the airplane and just content to be on the other side of something. One jumped onto my sleeve and stared at me with that blank expression airline passengers get from travel that isn't really flight. I set him on the lower wing and like a good passenger he didn't move. I wondered if he expected a safety lecture or a snack.

With the biplane in the sunlight I zipped up my jacket, climbed onto the same wing as the grasshopper, and gripping the handhold on the top wing I swung first one leg then the other into the cockpit before lowering myself onto the seat. It's that ritual open-cockpit entrance that separates this type of flying from everything else. There's no romance whatsoever to buckling a lap belt in seat 347D on a Chapter 11 airliner. Owning my own biplane may bankrupt me, but at least I'll feel like a pilot instead of payload. The grasshopper turned slightly to see if any other grasshoppers were coming along.

The engine start shuddered through the airframe like four kettledrums struck in quick succession. As I brought the throttle back to idle and leaned the mixture, I looked to the grasshopper who I'd swear now had goggles pulled onto his face to keep out the prop blast. Not being a grasshopper myself I left my goggles on my forehead and taxied to the runway.

As we—the grasshopper and I—lined up for takeoff, I pulled my goggles low, enriched the mixture, and slowly opened the throttle. The biplane shook and rolled forward. As the tail came up and I countered the left torque with a slight touch of right rudder I glanced to the wing where the grasshopper, who hadn't dislodged during the run-up, clung tenaciously to the fabric at 55…65…even 70 knots.

But I guess grasshoppers are only certified to 80 knots because as the wheels left the ground and the nose pitched up I looked past the airspeed indicator to give my passenger a thumbs-up, but he was gone. "Thank you...goodbye...thank you..."

Climbing in a right bank over a harvested bean field toward a rolling woodland beyond, I wondered if he'd go back to his grasshopper friends with word that there was a better way to get off the ground than by simply hopping. But then I glanced back at the tail and saw the fresh green splat on the horizontal stab. Sad, maybe, but perhaps it was better for him because all his non-pilot bug friends would just roll their bug eyes listening to him talk on and on about the glories of flying and they'd never get it.

© 2004

"Silly's Good"

Sean hadn't a clue what to do with his life, a condition he blamed on being 17. He was partially right and unaware that it'd take the remainder of his life to figure out the rest. Luckily, though, he'd run out of gas in the perfect spot for answers, far from anywhere he'd ever known. His car coasted onto the shoulder beside a fence, beyond which a field led to a squat metal building. There, with luck, he'd find gas and luckier still it'd be free. Sean had no idea how his fortune had changed as he tore his jeans on the fence's KEEP OUT sign and flopped into the weeds on the other side. He looked up just as an airplane lifted from beyond what he now realized were hangars. He couldn't know that as its shadow swiped over him it interrogated his soul like a radar beam, informing everyone on the airfield that an easy target approached.

"Run outa gas?" a voice called from inside the hangar behind a small, low-wing airplane.

"How'd you know?" Sean addressed a compact woman in mechanic's overalls emerging from the shadows.

"Only reason you'd be walkin' instead of drivin'." Her voice was pleasant but faded like burnt avgas. Deep lines creased a face weathered by years of airport sun. "Grab a rag," she said while pointing toward a cabinet where a dusty cat slept, coiled on top. "And don't wake Mr. Mulligan."

Confused, Sean started to ask about getting some gas but paused to examine the rose-colored airplane. With its canopy windows down, it resembled a winged sneaker. "What is it?"

"An airplane."

"What kind?"

"You'd know the difference?" And before Sean could turn to leave, the woman said, "Name's Katie…"

"What, the airplane?"

"No, me," she said through a smile. "I'm a flight instructor. The airplane's named, Clueless, on account of I had no clue what I was doin' when I bought her." Sean nodded, because he understood the feeling. Katie continued, "It's an Ercoupe—" She quickly held up a hand. "And no smart-mouth remarks about it lookin' like a playground toy. I like her. She flies sweet, and if you hope to get some gas you'll help clean her up." Again, Sean shrugged. At 17, it was his best conversational tool.

For the rest of the day, Sean polished the Ercoupe, running his hands along the slender fuselage and across its stubby wings. He giggled at the flat-footed pelicans Katie had painted on the twin rudders. "Okay, so it is silly looking," she admitted, and he replied, "Silly's good."

By late afternoon Sean was in the left seat with Katie in the other explaining how to start the engine. "You are 18, right?" she asked before pulling the starter handle. "Yeah," he lied, and she knew it. But if it took a lie to point another lucky kid toward the rest of his life in the sky, well, she'd have to remain clueless as she called, "Clear prop!"

© 2008

"Stealing Firsts"

When I opened the throttle he grabbed his head as though the prop blast would rip it off, which in an open-cockpit biplane it just might. Down the strip we rumbled, tailwheel drumming through rutted grass, dust swirled behind until four wings pulled us from the earth, and the newcomer in the front seat, still holding his head, flew for the first time.

"Ever been flying?" I'd always ask when guiding passengers across the lower wing and showing them how to grab the struts to climb into the front cockpit.

"Just in airlines," is the usual answer. And they somehow know that airline travel doesn't count as real flight; it's merely the bulk processing of human bone, blood, and baggage across a thousand miles to be extruded through jetways before rejoining life in another city that resembles the one they'd left behind two hours earlier.

"Step on the seat," I say to them from beside the fuselage, "And lower yourself down." They always hesitate. "Don't worry," I then add, "A little mud won't hurt the upholstery; your butt will wipe it clean for the next guy."

They giggle. Even the big guys with tattoos of ex-girlfriends' names fading on sun burnt biceps giggle. You can't help but giggle on a first flight, especially when it's taken in a biplane off a grass airfield in the middle of a place you never knew existed.

I slip first one and then the other strap over their shoulders and say, "Reach down to your side, there, and you'll find the lap belts." They do. I could just as easily say, "Reach down to your side, there, and you'll find a prairie rattlesnake." They'd still reach and pull the snake up by its tail, because once wrapped inside the fuselage they are mine to do as I say. They have no past, no connection to their comfortable reality that's already three feet below them. They've willingly decided to step into the sky through a portal that looks to them like the funny bi-wingers on the pizza boxes named for a WW I German ace who never ate the stuff. But it's the only image they have, and they trust pizza so what the heck? They grab the snakes, and I show them how to connect the straps into a harness, and with a snick of metal clasping metal latch themselves into the biplane's belly.

They feel proud knowing that, somehow, they're doing what few of their friends will ever do. Although, once they've flown they'll discover that most on the ground cannot understand what they've done. After this quick flight—whatever the impression—they'll be different from the rest of humanity, even if they never fly again.

Swinging my right leg over the rear cockpit rim, I'd said to my latest rider, "You might wanna turn that cap backwards; otherwise the wind'll tear it off." He did and clamped the headset across it. I settled into my seat, found the snakes, and with my own snick was ready to guide another ground-based human into first flight.

The engine shuddered to life, and wind swirled around us separating those on the sidelines from this guy in the front cockpit who could no more turn back now than Neal Armstrong could've looked at the moon and said, "Damn, that's one big step for this man, Buzz, you first!"

We taxied, and I checked the magnetos along the way, and then swinging the tail so I could scan the sky for traffic, I called, "Ready?" through the intercom, and he answered a flat, "Yeah." Had I said, "Banana-banana?" he would've answered likewise. The question was irrelevant; most are. His unspoken answer held it all: "Whatever it is I now face, I accept..." And I advanced the throttle so wheels rolled through a cloud of grass clippings as the biplane grabbed air and flew.

Sitting behind the passengers I never see their faces. They always look straight ahead until the wings change their lives from gravitational slaves to flyers. At about a hundred feet above the cornfield off the end of the runway, I watched him slowly rotate his head like a turtle cautiously poking out of its shell. Tentative, with a hand on the baseball cap as though holding in thoughts that now tried to burst from his overloading skull, he viewed the horizon and bravely looked below at what he expected would be his earth shrinking away but discovered, instead, the immensity of his own expanding mind. It happens every time; only the settings change.

If it's late afternoon the sky will slide them across a soft carpet of cool air. When midday thermals bump the wings knocking their heads from side to side I need to decide if it's too rough to continue, so over the intercom I'll casually ask, "Whaddya think?" Not, "Are you OK?" And if they can find the mic button the answer is usually, "Beautiful," "Awesome," or a visceral, "Wow," because there are no words for the first time your conscience gets ripped from its moorings and replaced by a chunk of glory that's been floating overhead your entire life.

I'll bank to point out landmarks, and as their minds adjust to the broad planet they'll spot something familiar and say, "My house...my school...(everything that I am), it looks so small." There's no fear and I envy their honest reaction to this dual reality inside the enormity of the flying universe with its ability to humble the tiny visitor whose mind frantically stretches to grasp the contradiction.

Regulations won't allow me to charge for the rides, but first-time flyers don't realize that I've already received my fee by stealing their first impressions, their clear vision of my world—a vision that oozes out of their uncontrollable smiles and giggling eyes. And as this passenger now walked away occasionally touching his head as though to keep the newfound images inside, I thought, "What a helluva way to not make a living."

© 2005

"Rudder, Rudder!"

"Rudder! Rudder! No, the other rudder!" I shouted as gently as possible into the student's ear.

"How much?" he asked.

"All ya got, just miss the cow…oh, never mind, she's moving." I looked back at a bovine rump bounding like a fat lady off a diving board. "Didn't know they could run that fast," I muttered and then turned my attention back to the runway. It swung left then right as Bob hammered first one rudder pedal and then the other in a valiant quest to keep the 1947 Cessna 140 running straight. We swerved in a squeal of burning rubber and CFI screams between lights. We clipped the soybean patch on the east side of the runway and headed for our second pass at the west edge corn. It was time for action, time for me to grab the bull by the nether region and act like a flight instructor. "Bob," I called.

"Name's George," he answered matter-of-factly.

"Corn is $2.04 per bushel, soybeans are $5.65…" I yelled as the windshield filled with tassels. "Pick one—corn or soybeans!"

And with that, George…Bob, or whoever he was beside me, hauled back on the control yoke. The underpowered, over-gross, two-seater built in the Truman Administration, shuddered. It groped for some trace of lift beneath its tired fabric wings. And like that scene in Flight of the Phoenix when the homebuilt barely clears the sand dunes, we barely cleared the $2.04-crop and flew.

"Corn it is," I exhaled. "You're doing fine, Bob."

"George."

And he could sense my panic recede as we climbed another 200 feet with every passing minute. Three-quarters of the Continental engine's 85 original horses wheezed beneath the cowling. Their

46

confident We-Think-We-Can hum reminded me of the VW minivan I drove cross-country after getting out of the Army. And then, an epiphany slammed into my brain like a bowl of cold Malt-O-Meal dropped from a Zeppelin: "Bob!" He barely looked. "Did you realize that the old Volkswagen engines are almost identical to what's driving this Cessna?"

Student pilots like it when the instructor distracts them from a routine lesson plan with mindless babble about the 1970s. "No," he said the way a Titanic passenger might've responded when the ship's captain noted over the PA: "And that scraping sound on your right is an iceberg. Funny, but three-quarters of an iceberg is submerged..."

Some days, I think that three-quarters of my flight instructor brain is submerged, but flight instructors can never stop learning, and I thank the heavens for sending me students to make it whole again.

© 2006

"Emily Flies Again"

She slipped the web harness over her shoulders, while I cautiously told her how to attach them to the lap belt. The trick, of course, was to convey the instructions without sounding like an instructor dad who still viewed his teenage daughter as a toddler in dress-up princess clothes—which, of course, being a dad, I do.

This was Emily's first ride in an open-cockpit biplane. Shortly after her birth I'd taken her flying in our Cherokee; strapped in a baby bucket we'd climb and swoop, and she'd gurgle and burp. By the time she was three, she flew our Aeronca from the front seat, although, mostly that consisted of yanking the joystick back and forth while squealing: "Eeee-yaaah..." By age nine, she no longer believed in princesses, and airplanes were something that Dad kept at the "boring" airport where old guys retold the same dull stories inside smelly hangars.

Then, on an unusually warm afternoon when the countryside had changed to gold beneath a sky so blue as to make a Crayola engineer squint, I was headed to the airport and asked—as I always do: "Emily, wanna fly the biplane?" With my hand on the door I expected her usual: "Ah, no thanks..." But, instead, she replied, "Sure."

One syllable broke through that long pause over the past half-decade. "Sure," and she grinned slightly, because teenagers aren't supposed to show excessive emotion to parents. She pulled a UC Santa Cruz sweatshirt over her head and said, "Let's go." I would've taken her hand—the one belonging to the three-year-old who used to fly with me—but I knew better.

Despite the time gap, she hadn't forgotten how to behave at the airfield. She stayed clear of propellers and helped remove the cockpit canopies and mousetraps from beneath the seats. Luckily, the trap lines were empty, the mice having learned it was safer to nest in the neighbor's Cessna 172 than inside the biplane.

"Pull on the strut," I said, and then tugging on the opposite wing, we rolled the Marquart Charger from its hangar. Sunlight—the unreal kind in late afternoon across dormant farmland—lit her face as no canned makeup ever could. "Now, hold your side while we swing the tail," and she understood how to turn the biplane until it pointed toward the grass runway.

It was a short but glorious flight across the few years that had separated us from her childhood to now, and as we landed—bounced—landed again, and taxied to the hangar, I anxiously awaited her approval as she would've awaited mine long ago.

She undid the harness, slipped the leather helmet from her head so the pony tail swung out, and then with a smile I'd waited to see for so long, she turned and replied to my, "So?" with, "I liked it..." And she pulled herself up by the top wing and just had to add: "Not much of a landing, though."

And that's my Emily, flying again at fourteen.

© 2005

"Back To School"

Hottest week of the year. Late summer, and the coastal hills were straw brown except where blackened from wild fires. Emily rolled through the airport gate, downshifting her Triumph TR6 motorcycle with a gentle clunk of the gearshift lever beneath her foot. The bark from the bullet mufflers echoed between the hangars. A mechanic waved from the maintenance shop where he'd been staring blankly into a Mooney's engine compartment. His posture saying, "Too much stuff crammed into such a tiny space."

Emily wheeled toward a hangar with its door open. A tall figure in shorts, tee-shirt and sneakers peeked around a Marquart Charger biplane. He didn't so much wave to Emily as signal, "I need you."

She coasted to a stop while lowering the kickstand like dropping retractable gear legs on a Bonanza. She dismounted and, in one smooth move, removed her helmet and shook her head. And that's when her father noted, "You cut it."

"Kept getting in the way," she answered and set her helmet over the mirror before removing her Belstaff jacket. Yeah, it was hot, but at 70 mph it'd felt appropriate. She walked around the biplane's nose where her father was attempting to reattach the cowling alone. Without asking, she took the loose end and held it so he could twist in the last screws.

"That should do it," he said and glanced at her. His blue eyes squinted the way only a father's can. "Your mother seen it yet?" Indicating her hair.

"She'll complain—"

"She'll get over it." He smiled, wiped his hands on a red shop rag and tossed it toward the workbench. It missed and joined several others on the floor. "All ready to go back?" He didn't smile asking that. Nor did Emily smile when she nodded, yes. "Good, let's push 'er out and see what you know."

With Emily on the right wing strut and her father on the left, they pulled the two-seat biplane from the hangar. The struts were warm and the asphalt sticky in the sunlight. A dry ocean breeze tried to move the windsock but quit after several anemic puffs.

"Take the back," he called. "I'll get the helmets." And he reached into a locker while Emily climbed onto the wing and then into the rear cockpit. She moved easily, as though on the motorcycle. Her father handed her a leather helmet and goggles before making the short climb into the front cockpit. Emily noticed how his knees slowed him, and how he left his helmet off until after she'd started the engine, just to feel the slipstream through his gray hair.

The next morning as she drove east in a car packed with books, clothes and Tupperware, Emily replayed her last flight of summer vacation. The wingovers, loops and spins were fun. But what made her hate to go back to school was the image of her father turning after she'd landed his biplane and saying, "Can't teach you nothing anymore." And his smile.

Chapter 5
Ghosts

"A Clear Vision"

One day I looked around the airport and noticed that everything had changed again. The light seemed brighter despite the approach of winter. The cornfield to the west was empty with a handful of Charolaise cattle munching their muddy way through the stubble, oblivious to me as I opened the hangar door. They didn't notice the windsock hanging limp against its post. They didn't care that summer had gone, that autumn had lost its reds and yellows and had lapsed into dull gold approaching dead brown. They just munched the stubble. Their similarity to people who never look up when an airplane flies over was uncanny. Pilots look up. Pilots walk off cliffs and drive into bridge abutments looking up at airplanes. We see things differently than cattle.

Unbuttoning the cowling I wondered if I should find the electric preheater and plug in the engine for a few hours before flying. I saw a mouse shoot from behind a can of butyrate dope on the gravel floor. She sensed my human presence, and then disappeared with a squeak that said, "You're busy, I'll come back later." Mice see airplanes differently than pilots.

Oil slid off the dipstick like the last words of a dying southern poet. Three and a half quarts of cold blood that couldn't care if I flew today or walked into the prairie and waited for the snows to cover me up. Oil has no compassion, no desire to be anything but what it is. Oil will never learn to fly.

The airplane's cockpit smelled of faded charts, dried avgas, and the ghosts of distant flyers who'd slid across the seats during the past half-century. Ghosts do leave a smell—more of an aroma, actually—inside old airplanes, and on cold autumn days, it condenses into that vague ether that permeates the cockpit.

Airplane ghosts aren't dead. They're what's left behind after a flight, each a unique shimmer of some marvel that popped into the flyer's mind as the wheels left the ground. Airplane ghosts never look inside logbooks to see who has the most hours and ratings. Instead, these spirits form wherever the human mind breaks free of the earth and completely surrenders to the invisible magic of flight. Airplane ghosts see lift where others see drag. They're impish, childish, and completely without discipline. They lure pilots into dusty hangars and taunt them to push airplanes into the bright sunlight.

As the cows munched across the stubble, and the mice peeked from behind their cracks in the baseboards, I swung the airplane's propeller. Ghosts jumped from magneto to sparkplug, exploding avgas and air inside cold cylinders. Heat blasted the autumn chill out the exhaust stacks as scores of Continental horses, each with a ghost rider on its back, howled for the sky.

Or at least that's how I saw it on a looming winter's day so clear that my normal vision just wasn't working properly. Luckily, the airplane ghosts took me aloft to keep it that way.

© 2002

"Closed Mondays"

Nick relit his cigar and sat atop the Taylorcraft's right wheel. Plucking a dandelion, he contemplated it and challenged, "Favorite air show pilot of all time." Adam paused from wiping oil off his motorcycle's crankcase before answering, "Hoover...no, Wagstaff...Wait! Tucker, definitely Sean Tucker...maybe...."

Nick blew smoke through the dandelion. Its seeds floated like tiny paratroopers silently dispersing around the wing into a timeless blue sky. "I seen him fly at Truckee-Tahoe back in the 1970s; stole the show."

"How come you never looped this thing?" Adam indicated Nick's airplane. "Never even seen you spin it."

Nick shrugged. "Not meant for aerobatics."

Adam shook his head. "Baloney! Erik Edgren does a great show in his T-crate." But Nick shot back, "That's a clipped-wing, completely different creature." Adam threw the oily rag at him, teasing, "Admit it, old man, you don't know how." Nick smiled and muttered, "Truth is I got dizzy upside down or spinning too many turns. Never got over it, so I just preferred to fly, watch the countryside and land wherever it looked inviting."

Adam slumped to the grass. Minutes escaped before he said, "Favorite airplane. If you could fly anything, what would it be?"

Nick didn't hesitate. "SPAD 13, then the Hawker Hurricane and..." He smiled, embarrassed.

"What?"

"You're gonna, think it's stupid."

"I think just about everything you say is stupid, never stopped you from saying it. What's your secret favorite airplane? F-86? DC-3…?"

"One-Fifty," Nick mumbled, and Adam stared as though he'd misheard. Nick stood and ducked beneath the wing brushing ash from his knee. "Yeah, the lowly Cessna 150." And as Adam laughed Nick continued, "I learned in one, taught in them, too. Developed sort of a soft spot for 'em." He studied the sprawling meadow with ankle-high grass undulating in a weak breeze off the nearby hills. "Getting late. Time to get back to the home."

Adam stood to gaze with him toward the lowering sun. "Wish you wouldn't call it that." Nick shrugged, snuffed his cigar against his boot heel and dropped it in the grass. Climbing into the Taylorcraft he called: "Give me a twist, and I'll race ya back."

Adam pulled the propeller through with one hand and stepped smoothly aside to mount the bike as the airplane's engine clacked to life. And by the time the Taylorcraft lifted, Adam leaned the motorcycle into a down-sloping turn, as both headed west.

Tuesday morning the curator unlocked the museum's door, removed the CLOSED MONDAYS sign and walked past the SPAD. Stopping at the Hawker Hurricane she checked the donation jar— empty. "Cheapskates," she muttered, and spotted a cold cigar butt between the museum's 1939 Taylorcraft and a dusty Indian motorcycle, both posed against a rolling meadow diorama. "If I ever catch whoever's…" Then she picked up the butt and left without seeing the mannequin at the Taylorcraft's controls grin toward his equally guilty friend on the bike. Nor could she see the dandelion seeds floating around their seemingly lifeless heads.

© 2011

"Mrs. Quimby Solos"

Fa-whapp! The old Skyhawk hit the runway and gut-punched the air from the instructor's lungs. It then staggered skyward and, defying Bernoullian logic, hung suspended like a cartoon figure contemplating imminent doom. Mathew groped for the throttle while yelling, "Power!" And as the wounded Cessna slowly climbed, he wheezed, "Watch your airspeed and, next time, begin the flare a tad closer to the runway…" Thinking: "Perhaps, below 50 feet."

Matthew knew he'd fallen for the oldest CFI trap—trusting the student who's nearing solo. Turning downwind, now, he felt the airplane slip and absently pointed at the coordination ball. Mrs. Quimby leveled the wings and then did something no student had done in the thousands of trips Mathew had made around that traffic pattern. She stopped—right there on downwind. Screech! Mathew bounced forward, pressing a hand to the instrument panel.

"Wha...what're you doing?" He swiveled his head confirming that, unbelievably, the airplane was parked in midair. "You can't stop here!"

"No?" Quimby unbuckled her seat belt. "I'm not getting much out of you, so I'm leaving." She opened the door. Mathew expected a rush of air to press it back, but it swung easily as though still on the ground. His student climbed past the landing gear and closed the door behind her while giving a friendly wave. Mathew pleaded, "Get back inside...you can't solo without me—"

"Can't I?" Quimby interrupted and stepped forward of the leading edge to stand 800 feet above the earth. A Stearman suddenly flew past, its shadow flashing through the cockpit. Mathew ducked. Quimby smiled and turned to him, "I get the impression your heart's no longer with me. You're going through the motions rather than actually teaching, let alone flying."

"Not so," Matthew defended himself and leaned to talk through the open window. Looking down, he recoiled. Like many pilots, he was afraid of heights but always felt secure buckled inside an airplane at any altitude. He turned back to his student who now sat Buddha-like in the sky. "Will you, please, get back inside? This looks bad."

"Not until you get your heart back inside the cockpit," Quimby replied. "I expect a fully engaged instructor. You let me slam that last one on without intervening."

Matthew shot back, "You're close to solo, so I have to let you make your own way."

"Then, you admit it's time."

Mathew hesitated and whispered, "You aren't ready."

"Who isn't ready—you or me?"

"I can't be here with you forever." He indicated the cockpit, which was absurdly quite behind a dead engine. The only sounds were the wind and distant murmur of the Stearman turning final. Mrs.

Quimby hesitated and then stood. When she lightly caressed the wingtip and blew him a kiss the engine restarted. Then, with air rushing through the window, Matthew Quimby felt his wife's presence leave him forever, one year after she'd died. And, crying, alone, he knew that his favorite—and most difficult student—had soloed at last.

© 2009

"Where'd You Go?"

Bill swung the Piper Super Cruiser's tail in a half-arc stopping just above the tiedown rope. Barely had the rudder straightened when the propeller ticked to a stop and the side door popped open. A seatbelt clanked against the floorboards and Bill slipped from the airplane. He wiped his bald scalp with the same hand that held his seed corn cap, then pushed the cap back on and walked from beneath the wing with the gait of a flyer who's been somewhere.

"Where'd ya go?" I asked from beneath my engine as I tried again to align a sparkplug into its dark hole. For reasons known only to the gods top plugs go in nicely, and bottom plugs always cross-thread.

"Over to Sigourney," Bill said and sat on an overturned five-gallon paint can to watch without looking.

"Anything happening over there?"

He thought and then answered, "Nellie said she was annualing a Tri-Pacer that Glen's puttin' up for sale."

"It look any good?"

Bill shrugged—could've been a yes, might've been a no. The point of the flight hadn't been to shop for airplanes; he'd just been out flying, keeping alive that often forgotten art of simply going somewhere that really wasn't a destination. His 100-hp Super Cruiser was the perfect just-flying machine for him. With a tank of gas he could explore half of Iowa or wander into southern Minnesota as easily as a spring cloud moving across the prairie.

Inside the cockpit you'd find a couple of out-of-date sectional charts tucked into a pouch with a few pencils, a flashlight, and a packet of cheese 'n crackers—the pilot essentials.

Bill was a private pilot, the kind who worked five days each week so he could spend Sundays at the airfield. His logbook would never read in the thousands of hours, but if you included the time spent patching fabric, chasing corrosion, changing oil, gapping plugs, or wiping grease from the airplane's belly, Bill's aviation experience would easily rival the best.

As our flying world tries to redefine itself by constantly impressing us with its ability to complicate the familiar, we should take a moment to look around the ramp, to peek into the dim hangars where the unseen flyers keep the small dreams quietly alive. Each hangar is a museum dedicated to lives spent in search of the peace that only wings can bring. Each pilot is an explorer who may not lead followers into new territories, but instead the private pilot who flies between air shows and free pancake feeds is the pioneer who seeks the grander view.

Inside their flying machines these people named Bill and Nellie and Glen may look like anyone else, but they harbor greatness. They have that unique ability to float on the wind to wherever their spirits call. They're you and me, and when they land we need to ask, "Where'd you go?" And then listen, because Bill, Nellie, and Glen have since gone west, and that only leaves us to answer.

© 2002

"In a Lifetime"

"It's called a Warner Sportster," Joseph muttered from beneath the airplane's engine.

"Looks like a Flybaby," Franklin noted and tapped his pipe against the monoplane's low wing.

"Well, it's not…and, please don't do that."

Franklin ignored him. "Maybe a P-26. Got that P-26 Peashooter look with the open cockpit and radial engine." He watched Joseph torque a spark plug into a bottom cylinder where oil dripped onto a floor pan. And even though Joseph was doing his best to ignore the old man, Franklin persisted: "So, what inspired you to mount a Rotax engine on this thing? Plans called for a Continental."

Joseph visualized blood oozing from his tongue as he bit down while choosing his words. "I've told you before; it's a Rotec, not Rotax, and I like how it looks." Then he stood and nudged past his kibitzing visitor. "Excuse me."

Franklin stepped aside, set his pipe on the workbench and watched Joseph press both hands against the base of the tail's flying wires. "Finally going to fly it?"

Joseph nodded, yes, and Franklin offered an uninspiring, "Think you're ready?" Joseph shook his head, no, then, yes, and pushed on the tail.

Franklin leaned against the workbench as the little homebuilt rolled past. The morning sky was cool but would burn when the sun crested the mountains, sending rattlesnakes looking for shade.

"You know," Franklin opined, "A guy could rig up a motorized device and attach it to the gear legs so's you wouldn't have to put all that pressure on the flying wires." Joseph shot him a side-glance, but Franklin shrugged, "Merely thinking out loud. It's your airplane, wouldn't want to tell you how to handle it."

Joseph mumbled, "Yeah you would."

"Don't have to get all sensitive about it. I'm just making a few observations. A guy should be willing to take some constructive advice."

Joseph sighed and had to agree, but when he turned to offer an apology it was too late. Franklin was gone. Joseph leaned against the airplane and squinted at a timeless sky. It looked as it had years before when his father gave him his first flight in the J-3 Cub that now sat in the rear of the hangar. Joseph panned through the decades to a gap at the workbench where he'd once stood beside Franklin and unfolded a set of plans. With the naïve enthusiasm of a young man who'd never built an airplane he'd said, "It's called a Warner Sportster, Dad."

Now, as Joseph lifted the dusty pipe from the workbench the cold aroma of spent tobacco rekindled images of his father's blue eyes studying those plans. "Looks like a Flybaby," the memory said and tapped the pipe onto a wing drawing before brushing cold ashes onto the floor. "But I suppose we'd better get started building if you plan to finish this thing in my lifetime."

Later, when Joseph flew the wings he'd built with his father, he looked skyward and said, "One lifetime wasn't nearly enough."

(In memory of James Franklin Berge 1923-2011)

"Goodnight, Sun"

It resembled a molten volleyball suspended above the ocean as though hesitant to call it a day. Hal slid his RV-3's canopy back and squinted against the sun's heat reflecting off the silver wing. It warmed his face while accenting decades of creases formed in the sky. And even though he lingered preflighting an airplane he'd owned for ten years, the sun never moved. It just hung like a stage light awaiting his entrance.

Everyone knew Hal, but no heads turned on the ramp as his single-seater lifted from the runway and leveled momentarily to gain speed before pulling away in a banking turn. No head except one. And that pilot climbed into a biplane, twisted her cap backwards and started the engine. By the time Beth took the runway the RV-3 was a glittering firefly teasing the sunset. She watched it climb and kick its tail sideways before dropping into a wingover. Gaining speed, again, it pitched up to place its nose slightly above the horizon before slow rolling like a lazy football.

Beth kept a short distance from the RV-3, watching it snap and loop above the water. The pilot's face was indistinct beneath a canopy glowing in solar fire. But she knew the face, could paint it in her sleep and pictured it grinning to tempt her in. All the while she climbed in a circle until well above him. Then, convinced he'd had too much fun alone, she dove with the sun at her back. "Hey, old man," she started to call, but he felt her approaching and pulled up sharply to roll off the top of a half-loop.

"Immelmann," she laughed and followed him into another dive, the flying wires buzzing against the wind. And she chased him down until they flew above the waves where a pair of surfers vanished through a watery tube.

Time hung suspended with the sun above the ocean as Beth and Hal flew rings around each other. Neither out flew the other, and both enjoyed their opponent's mastery of the sky. He easily out ran her but hung back just enough for Beth to feel as though she could catch him. Until, finally, the sun budged from its perch, and her fuel gauge said it was time to land. In a gentle bank with her eyes straining into the last burst of daylight she watched the RV-3 draw beside her framed between wing tips and struts. Its silhouette faded in purple flame when the pilot waved, pulled up and banked away. Gone.

Later, after she'd landed and climbed from the cockpit, Beth removed her cap, shook out her gray hair and stood for a moment. The unforgiving silence of the Hawaiian sunset thundered inside her head before she pushed her biplane inside the hangar. Turning, she ran her fingertips across the dusty RV-3 in the corner and whispered, "Good night, old man," because she couldn't say good bye. Only then did the sun drop onto the sea for another night.

© 2010

"Memorial Day"

The pilot lounge regulars refilled coffee mugs before heading to the porch outside the UNICOM office. Chuck brought the glass jar and leaned against a post as the others—Ed, Johnny and Bill—lined up along the railing.

"That him?" Chuck asked, squinting into the sunrise. The others nodded and watched a Cessna 150 descend on base leg. It was Elwood. Every Memorial Day morning for the past fifteen years he'd take off before dawn, circle the bay and return before the sky filled with holiday flyers. And every few years the judges' panel added a new member, there to rate his landings.

"I say two bounces," Johnny said after looking toward the windsock. He tossed a nickel into the jar.

"At least three, and he won't make the second turn-off," Ed offered and added his nickel.

Chuck spit over the railing and growled, "I say he don't even make it and has to go 'round." He added a dime.

Bill lifted his baseball cap to run his fingers through thin gray hair before saying, "You're all too pessimistic. I'll take those bets." He tossed a quarter into the jar. "The kid knows how to fly."

The others grunted and watched Elwood's Cessna glide toward the runway. "Too high," Johnny said. "Won't get it down." Chuck smiled adding, "Never make it flying Liberators."

Johnny snorted, "Anyone can fly something with four engines; real test is in the P-47." And the friendly argument between the old vets barely got off the ground when Elwood pulled on the last notch of flaps and pointed the nose down.

"Looking better," Bill teased, and the others said nothing as the 150 flared just above the threshold. Elwood held the airplane's nose high and gently touched on the mains. After the nose wheel reached the pavement, the Cessna turned at the first intersection and taxied toward the office.

"Well, willya look at that," Johnny muttered.

"Maybe the kid can fly," Ed added as Chuck extended the winnings jar to Bill who waved it away saying, "Be wrong to take money from Air Force fools who can't judge a real pilot."

"What's a Navy jock know about flying, anyhow?" Chuck laughed, and Ed jumped in, "Hey, don't bad mouth the Navy!" And they laughed as Elwood walked from his airplane up the steps, passing them without a word. And just as silently they followed him into the pilot lounge where he picked up his coffee mug with the Cobra helicopter painted on the side. Hesitating, he stared at four dusty mugs turned upside down on the upper shelf. Softly, he read each name: "Chuck," as though addressing the inverted B-24 on the cracked mug, "Johnny," and the P-47's blunt nose, "Ed" and an SNJ banking above a blue ocean. Finally, "Bill" the most recently added mug showed a P2V above a map of Japan. Beside it stood a coin-filled glass jar. Then, just like every Memorial Day, Elwood saluted and confessed that he missed them all.

© 2010

"The Fuselage"

He drove a '59 Rambler. It first appeared at the airport when Terry bought the old Waco fuselage, hauled it to the airport on a flatbed trailer and set it at the north end of the hangars in the weeds.

"What is it?" I asked.

"A Waco, Taperwing Waco," Terry answered. "Bought it at a farm auction in Nebraska."

"Where's the rest of it?" There was only the uncovered airframe and vertical fin. The gear legs were attached but bent and without wheels.

"That's all I got."

"No wings? No engine?" I barely hid my amusement.

"No," he said defensively. "Don't need more. I can rebuild it with what's there...and some plans...and a little scrounging."

And that's how it stayed throughout the year. The only one ever going near it was the old man who drove the Rambler. He'd turn up at twilight and always parked his car near a spot in the fence where the posts leaned over, drooping the barbed wire to the ground, making it easy for him to step over and walk slowly to the old biplane's fuselage. He had to be well over 90, I guessed, although he seemed in good health. At first, I thought he was just another stranger out to watch airplanes fly and simply chose that spot near the Waco to remain unobtrusive. Soon, however, I noticed he never watched us fly, preferring, instead, to stare at the derelict fuselage.

He did more than stare at it, his eyes moving as though taking inventory of what was left in the rusted structure, and I thought I saw him talking to the fuselage or talking with someone that I couldn't see. Throughout the winter, he'd appear before sunset, park the Rambler beside the fence, then pick his way through the dead weeds and snow around the fuselage—always studying it. He never looked anywhere else and never at me. His hands would occasionally reach out to touch the rusty airframe, and then as if he stood beside a complete biplane with engine and wings attached, he would nod his head in some sort of approval of something else I couldn't see.

I moved closer to him one snowy afternoon and stood within hearing distance at the edge of a hangar. The air was cold and still as the inside of a closet. Snow collected on his thin shoulders and wide-brimmed hat. It coated the airframe's tubing in fuzzy rails. His breath rose in weak puffs, indicating he was speaking. I strained to hear, but his voice was too thin. It sounded as though he issued instructions to someone unseen. Then he patted the fuselage with an approving smile and shuffled toward the Rambler, taking, I assumed, his unseen companion with him

"Hey, Terry," I asked one afternoon inside the shop. "Have you ever seen that old guy who comes out here poking around the Waco?"

"What old guy?" Terry answered from beneath a customer's airplane.

"Some guy hangs around...You haven't seen him?"

"No, I don't get down that end of the field, too busy." He dropped a wrench, and it rang sharp against the concrete floor, punctuating his suspicion: "Why?"

"Oh, just wondering," I said. "He seems, I don't know, peculiar, that's all."

"You see any weirdoes around here, you chase them off. Airports always seem to attract weirdoes, somehow. Don't know what it is about them."

Spring came, snow left, yellow flowers grew thick around the derelict fuselage, and the Rambler continued to show up at sunset. I was busy flight instructing for Terry, hoping to save enough money to pay for my Airline Transport Pilot's license. A rumor had spread that the airlines were hiring—the one's that weren't bankrupt—and the fever had me. I had to build hours, so day after day I slogged around the pattern, repeating the same speeches about airspeed and coordination to my faceless students. In spite of me, they learned to fly, and I accumulated hours toward my airline goal.

The days lengthened, the air turned warm, and the Rambler parked alongside the fence almost daily. I watched the old man for a few seconds at a time with each pass we'd make on a touch-and-go. For several days, he confined himself to the airplane's nose, pointing at the firewall and its empty motor mounts. Just as he had directed his imaginary companion around the nonexistent wings throughout the winter, he now assisted in overhauling an engine that wasn't there. He even dragged an old wooden crate beside the fuselage and stood on it to reach where the tops cylinders would be, if there had been any, which there weren't.

"Hey, Terry, that old guy's back. You ought to see him. He thinks he's putting an engine on the Waco."

"Uh-huh," Terry muttered without looking up from a stack of fuel receipts. "I thought I told you to keep the weirdoes out."

"I don't think he's causing any trouble, it's just...."

"Uh-huh. Don't you have a student waiting outside?"

Around and around I droned in the traffic pattern through bad landing after bad landing. "Watch your airspeed; hold more rudder next time; correct for the wind, keep that wing down, use that adverse aileron yaw to your advantage. Okay, let's go around and try it again." The words fell from my mouth like so much nonsense from a parrot. Then, down the narrow airstrip, back into the sky, and each evening before sunset the Rambler would appear on the gravel road, stop beside the fence, and the old man would walk slowly through the wildflowers to work on his biplane. I had to consider it his; no one else went near it.

"Hey, Susan," I interrupted a student one afternoon, tapping her shoulder as we lifted off. "Do you see that old guy over there?"

"Where?" she responded in near panic. "Sorry! I didn't see him; did I hit him?"

"No, he's by the hangar."

"Dead?"

"No. Alive...I think. See?"

"Huh?"

"No, back behind us now. Oh, it's too late, you can't see him now. Watch your airspeed, let's climb on up to three thousand feet." I made a note never to interrupt Susan with my stray observations while she was concentrating on landing.

Spring folded into summer, and the yellow flowers around the fuselage gave way to fat grass and thistle full of bees and mice. I managed to get my airline license and then picked up the occasional charter flight hauling chickens mostly. Flying from dawn until after dark, the hours piled up in my logbook, and by mid-summer all I could think about was getting on with the airlines. My application was in, so I waited and continued to drag around the pattern in worn-out Cessnas looking for the old man to arrive each afternoon to put in his time with the Waco.

"Are you sure you've never seen him?" I asked Terry one morning before the first student arrived. "He's down there every evening."

"What's his name?" Terry asked pouring a saucer full of evaporated milk for the airport cat.

"I don't know, I've never met him, I'm always busy when he comes out, but you must have seen him."

"No," Terry snapped. "I've more important things to do than sit around chatting with airport groupies who've got more time than they know what to do with, so they sit out here drinking my coffee, watching me work and my airplanes fly without ever buying anything."

"But he doesn't watch them fly," I said. "He just stays with the Waco...like...like he was rebuilding it or something."

"Has he been dinking around with my fuselage?"

"No, he really doesn't do anything, that's my point. He *thinks* he's doing something."

"All right," Terry said standing. "Let's go down right now and meet this nut case."

"He's not there now, he only shows at sunset." Terry shook his head and disappeared into the shop. I heard something drop and his muffled voice complaining. My first student drove up and the sun rose over the trees.

That evening as a thunderstorm rumbled to the east, and the ground steamed from the shower that had just passed over, I stood outside the office inhaling the beautiful moment that doesn't exist anywhere else but on a small airport when the sky is soft and sounds like old dreams. My back ached from sitting all day in cramped cockpits. A Cessna 150 crawled overhead, approaching to land, its engine a murmur against the distant thunder.

I looked along the hangar row and saw the Rambler's grill poking through the weeds. The old man, silhouetted by the orange sun, was inside the Waco's rear cockpit, seated on an overturned bucket, moving his head from side to side. He'd stare at the blank instrument panel, then leaned out, calling to someone near the propeller—only, of course, there was no one near the propeller, and there was no propeller on this wingless, motorless, skeleton biplane.

I looked around and except for the Cessna turning final I was alone. Terry had run into town, and my next flight, a charter, was not due for fifteen minutes, so I went to finally meet the old man in the Waco. I made it as far as the second hangar when Terry's truck drove into the parking lot beside a gray Cadillac. He hurried toward me, calling: "Your charter's here." My passengers walked toward the Piper Seneca while talking on cellphones with that I'm-very-important look that indicates that they have nothing to say and only talk on cellphones in hopes someone will acknowledge their being.

"What are you waiting for?" Terry asked. "Get their bags...and smile."

I glanced toward the Waco before turning back. The old man motioned toward his phantom assistant while shaking his head. Apparently, the Waco's imaginary engine had refused to start. "Did you see him?" I called back to Terry, but he was already inside the office.

With autumn a week away, Terry was mowing the weeds around the Waco. The flail mower cut even circles around the old airframe, chewing up thistle and grass into dying summer's pulp. I hadn't seen the Rambler for a week and missed the old man's presence at twilight. The sun dropped below the horizon, and the air cooled as Terry parked the tractor in its shed, and I went home.

Mixed in with the usual mail that evening was a thick envelope from the airlines. I tore into it dropping a handful of forms onto the kitchen table. I read the cover letter, hoping to spot the key phrase somewhere in the standard organizational format. There it was: "Please notify this office no later than 15 October to schedule an interview...." I was in—well, almost. No more students or charters, I was going to work for the airlines. One day it might even pay more than flight-instructing.

That night I barely slept and was out to the airport before dawn. The air was cool, and the wind calm across a rosy sky. The runway lights flickered pale yellow in the linen wisps of ground fog, and I walked through the dew-covered grass in what I thought was a random route but actually lead toward the Waco. Fate giggled at my notions of self-control when I heard a deep clacking rumble slap at the morning air. An engine started, a large engine, definitely not one of the Cessnas or even the Seneca, which I knew was still inside the hangar. Someone advanced the throttle, and what sounded like a radial engine growled from around the last hangar, echoing into the dawn.

I hurried as the sun broke above the treetops turning autumn into a firestorm of yellows and lavender. The radial's call, a vicious drum line, was now intense as I turned the corner of the last hangar, and a sparrow shot past my face from beneath an eave. I swatted, then stood with arms limp at my side staring at a full, all-black biplane with furnace-red trim, its radial engine swinging a long silver propeller that caught the sun's early rays in a flashing pinwheel of dream light.

It was, of course, the Waco Taperwing that had no wings. Only, now it did, and a tail, and tires, plus a radial engine, and a woman who looked like dawn itself as she smiled from the front cockpit. The sunlight was sucked into the ebony fabric and exploded back in resonant glory, accented by the red trim that looked too hot to touch. Atop this flaming vision a tall figure in leather swung into the rear cockpit. But before he settled into his seat he turned toward me. The sun lit his face in that same red that fired the sky, but, even in shadow, I would've known who it was—the old man from the Rambler.

It was his face but sixty years younger; the hair full, curly, and dark. His shoulders were broad, arms and legs quick. He waved, smiled, and pulled a leather helmet over his ears but left the straps dangling. Squinting against the sight, I barely returned his wave when he opened the throttle, and the Waco taxied past me in a symphony of wind and power. Then ignoring the paved runway, it bounced across the grass and lifted into the dawn sky. With a wave from both occupants, it banked and vanished in a tapering finale of unearthly light and sound.

The runway lights clicked off as Terry's pickup turned onto the gravel road toward the office. For several minutes, I stared at the now empty sky then turned back to where the Waco had been. The weeds were evenly cropped where Terry had mowed but stood in a ragged V forming the shape of the now missing fuselage. The sun rose higher. Dawn faded into daylight, and I looked beyond the weeds and the fence to the Rambler parked alone and empty.

Terry appeared by my side.

"Where the blazes is my Waco?" he bellowed.

"I...I don't think it was ever yours," I said and walked toward the car. And, there on the dashboard was a key, the car's title signed by the owner, and a note to me: *Hey Kid. Pump the accelerator twice on a cold day, and she starts fine. It's a boring car, but looks as though you're heading into a boring life unless you remember what you saw here.*

And I tossed the key back on the dash and walked away realizing that I had a long way to go before I learned how to fly.

© 1987

"The Logbook"

The double beam from atop the control tower cut through the frozen gloom in tireless strokes—green, white; green, white.... Yellow flashes from the hazard lights on the snowplows moved slowly along the runway.

Vernon had just slid his car off the access road in front of the cargo terminal when he pushed his sleeve up to read his watch—1:38 a.m. Except for the handful of snowplows, the airport was quiet. The last airliner would have landed at midnight, and the nightly cargo flights, a collection of just about anything with engines, wings and a vacuous hole for cargo, would arrive around 3 a.m. The pilots were all young. They hauled everything from canceled checks to lobster tails. It was aviation at its most raw. Vernon, by contrast, hadn't flown since losing his medical certificate on his 66th birthday.

It was a short distance to the terminal—the old terminal, not used for passengers since the early 1970's. There was a newer one made of glass across the field for the airlines. Vernon worked in the old brick terminal, now used exclusively for cargo.

After trying the car door, held shut by a snowdrift, he crawled over the gearshift and brake handle and out the passenger's side. He slammed the door, catching his coat and lost his balance on the ice.

"Whaaa....Umph!"

His right elbow struck the frozen pavement with a sharp jab, and he wallowed in the slush, tangled in his overcoat. Vernon pushed himself to his feet and walked stiffly toward the old terminal. The snow changed back to sleet. By the light of the street lamps he saw his reflection in the glass doors. A stocky old man in a baggy overcoat, he thought, then squared his shoulders and moved the cigar from one corner of his mouth to the other.

His elbow throbbed from the fall, but the rest of his body felt strong. Watching his reflection through the rain, he remembered the first day he had walked up to the terminal, decades earlier. Recently discharged from the Navy after two years in the Pacific, flying Martin PBM flying boats, he was just another pilot looking for a job. The offer of $30 per week and a room had brought him to the Midwest. Fifty years of life since then had kept him there.

He pushed the door open and shook the sleet from his hat.

"Evening, Vern," a sleepy voice from behind the dispatcher's counter called.

"Hmmm," Vernon grumbled. The room was warm, stuffy warm. The smell of coffee and cigarettes made it lonely.

"Is it snowing yet?"

"Started to," Vernon answered. "Mostly sleet. Got stuck in a snowbank." He waved vaguely at the parking lot.

"One of the plows can pull you out later."

"Umm," Vernon grunted. A radio played music somewhere in a darkened corner. Vernon stepped around a pile of cinder blocks and boards in the center of the room. "Haven't they started remodeling in here yet?" he asked looking around at the gutted old building.

"No, just deposited more junk."

He ignored the answer and went into the men's room. Looking at himself in the cracked mirror above the sink he decided his face was the same—the same one he had brought in 1947. There were more lines, of course, and parts sagged where once they had been tight, but it was the same face staring back. He ran his hand across his short wavy hair. "Cab Calloway's hair," he said and laughed.

Suddenly, a toilet flushed behind him, and a stall door swung open with a long squeak. "What'd you say?" One of the mechanics emerged buttoning his insulated overalls, an amused smirk on his lips.

"Huh?" Vernon started. "Oh, my hair." He pointed, embarrassed. "My wife used to say I had Cab Calloway's hair."

"Who?"

"Cab...a band leader. Before your time."

The mechanic left, and Vernon glanced around at the battered tile walls, steam radiator and heavy porcelain fixtures. "Old," he sighed. "Old and worn out." He rubbed his sore elbow, tossed the cold cigar butt into a urinal and strode out. He glanced down the long dark hallway, past the empty stalls where Frontier, Braniff, and Tri-State Airlines had all had their ticket counters. At the end of the hall was the empty operations office and the old flight school; all long gone.

"The Mitsubishi flying 321 is stuck in Omaha. I thought I could get the Cheyenne on 308 to swing over there from Kansas City and...."

Vernon cut the dispatcher's voice off with a wave. "Give me ten minutes," he said and disappeared into his office, a tiny room across from where the hangar had been. He closed the door behind him and stood in the dark, staring out the window.

He missed the hangar—missed it terribly. He missed many things. He missed his wife. He missed flying. He missed being a child and listening to the mail planes fly over his house toward the night beacon, flashing steady white every ten seconds. He massaged his elbow. The control tower's rotating beacon swept green and white overhead. He looked out where the hangar had been. It was almost completely gone now, only the one wall remained, and as soon as the weather cleared it, too, would go. A bulldozer sat posed, waiting.

He flicked on the light. A cluttered desk, a single file cabinet, the radiator and a phone—these were his tools. On one wall were two photographs. He lit another cigar. Blue smoke rose toward the ceiling. He stepped closer to the wall and stared. One photograph showed the nose of a Martin PBM towering above a small cluster of young men in casual Navy uniforms. Everyone smiled, including the short officer with the wavy hair dressed in tee shirt and cap and cigar clamped arrogantly between his teeth. Someone had scrawled: "With Love, From, Iwo Jima—1945" across the picture.

The other photograph had been taken beside the now demolished hangar outside his office. It showed a pair of Aeronca Champs drawn nose to nose and a wedding party in tuxedos and gowns arranged in a crescent in front of the planes. All the faces were young and happy, including the young groom with the black wavy hair and his bride. "Chief Pilot and Squaw—June 1948"

The door swung open behind him, and the aroma of coffee flowed in with the dispatcher.

"I go home now," the dispatcher said. "I sent 308 to Omaha to pick up 312's load; your first flight's due in at 3:16 a.m.; 308 will be in at 3:45; 312, when they fix it, will go back to Kansas City; the runway's been glycol'd; I hear one of Night Express's went off the runway at Minneapolis—so much for the competition; the coffee's fresh; we need sugar, and there's only three thousand gallons of Jet fuel, more should be delivered tomorrow if it doesn't snow. Good Night."

Vernon followed him out.

"What's this?" Vern asked picking up a dusty black book from the counter.

"That? Oh, one of the construction workers found it this morning when they tore out a wall..." He pointed toward the old hangar. "It's someone's logbook—old, real old. I was going to toss it out." With that he left.

Vernon turned the logbook over slowly in his hands. The binding was dry and cracked. It opened with a gentle rustle. The musty smell of the years rose to his nostrils sending a sharp pang through his emotions. He read the name: Charles S. Dansig. It meant nothing. The wind blew suddenly, rattling snow against the plate windows like thousands of tiny claws. Vernon looked up and reached for the thermostat, turning it a notch higher. He took the logbook into his office. He sat at his desk and read the name in the logbook again: Charles S. Dansig. It was taking on a familiar ring. He thought a moment, staring out the window past the bulldozer now fuzzy with snow. A thought dawned. He glanced at the two photographs on the wall. In one lunge he moved from behind his desk to the wall and lifted the Navy picture from its nail. The light was pale, so he twisted the desk lamp's neck, pointing it at the wall.

"Dansig," he said to himself. "Charlie Dansig, I've heard that name, I know it."

Turning the photograph over, he fumbled with the staples holding the cardboard back to the frame. One of the staples was brittle and snapped, making a neat incision in his right index finger. A drop of blood soaked into the cardboard.

The photograph slid easily from the frame. He moved closer to the lamp and turned the glossy print over. The same fountain pen that had scrawled across the picture's face listed the crew's name starting with the plane's commander, Vernon L. Ackerbach, Lt., USN. Vernon scanned down the list, but the only name close to Dansig was, Charles "Charlie Horse" Danbury, a gunner. He set the print down on the glass frame and stared into the snow. The green and white arms of the beacon swept through the dusty night. He turned back to the wall, looking at the wedding photo. One by one, he examined the party, naming the young figures. "Harold Reynolds, Susie Hickok, Trevor Hedges...." He paused briefly and stared at his late wife, her round face smiling and bright; the white lace cascading across her dark hair. He said her name, "Peggy."

Suddenly, he looked to the end of the line and saw a tall, older man, dressed in a tuxedo the same as the others. The figure smiled like the others, but Vernon had forgotten his name. He flipped the picture over and tore the photograph from its mount, reading the back. Again the names were listed, but nothing even close to, Charles S. Dansig. The forgotten man was, Daniel Jones, a pilot Vernon had known and forgotten long ago. Dejected, he sat behind the desk and pushed the dismantled frames away. Their presence in the old building across from the old hangar depressed him. He watched the snow, then turned back to the desk, adjusted the lamp, and reached for the logbook.

With little interest, he flipped through the yellow edged pages reading the entries. They began in 1929 and ended abruptly in late 1931. Several blank pages followed the last entry. Vernon leaned over the desk. This was apparently Dansig's second logbook. He estimated him to have almost 2000 hours when it terminated in 1931; almost a thousand of that coming in the last two years. The entries were scribbled, some in pen, others in dull pencil. Daily entries had been abandoned at the very beginning of the book, the owner choosing to lump weekly totals together in single line entries. Apparently, Charles S. Dansig flew the mail. Almost all the logged time was in a Boeing 40 biplane, one of those huge mail carriers Vernon remembered seeing as a boy.

He recalled sneaking off at night with his brother, Leonard, riding double on the bicycle to the airport in Salt Lake City to watch the airmail planes come in. Nobody had bothered them as they stood in the dark arguing over which was better, the open cockpit Boeing 40's or the great model 80's, the tri-motor biplanes—*Pioneer Pullmans of the Air*. His brother leaned toward the later, while Vernon argued the merits of having one's head out in the wind where one could feel the sky. A stab of loneliness rocked him, thinking of his brother. He tried not to think of the dead, but the memories came flooding back.

Slowly, he reached for the photographs, choosing the wedding picture. He stared at the group, the two Aeroncas and the date, June 7, 1948. He remembered how the wedding had been delayed a year after his brother's death. He wanted to cry but refused. He slid the photograph away from him and picked up the logbook again. "Well, Mr. Dansig, how did you manage to lose this?"

That's when he noticed the radio was silent, the music gone. A low hum of static hissed through the halls. He glanced at his watch, 2:30 a.m. "Must have gone off the air," he mumbled and stood.

Outside the office he snapped the radio off. At the far end of the hallway, where the flight school had been, a fluorescent bulb flickered, trying to die. Wind rattled something deep inside the building. Vernon shivered from the cold. "Impossible to heat this damn place," he said.

He walked down the long empty hall toward the flickering bulb, his own footsteps sharp against the cold stone floor. Looking at his hand, he noticed he still carried the logbook.

"Mmm," he uttered and reached for the light switch outside the old flight school office, and hesitated.

The school had been gone since 1951 when he last instructed there. Since then it had been used as an operations room, a maintenance office; an insurance company had even leased it for two years. Lately, it had been used for storage. Vernon peered inside and snapped on a light—four walls, all yellow, and a mop and bucket. Nothing remained of the hundreds of young men who passed through on the G.I. Bill. There was no trace of the maps, the training aids, the posters. Vernon stepped inside. He turned to his right, to exactly where the counter had stood, where Peggy had stood. He saw her. At least he felt as though he could see her.

"Hello," he said shyly. The cold walls stared back. "New skirt? I like plaid...Doing anything after work? No? I just got paid, care to...You would? Great! I have a student, now," he said aloud. "I'll see you when..." He heard his excited voice echo in the empty room and froze. He turned abruptly, leaving the room after smacking the light switch off. The fluorescent bulb still flickered as he strode back along the empty hallway toward his office.

"Stupid," he mumbled. "Forget them...Gone...They're all gone."

He rounded the corner into his office and gathered the photographs in one hand trying to take the frames as well. He still carried the logbook. *Smash!* The two glass frames hit the floor and shattered, the shards dispersing under the desk and chair.

"Ahhh..." He bent to pick up the broken frames, then stood. "You can stay there!" he shouted. "You belong there!" He turned toward the snow and felt his eyes swell. "You left me here," he said quietly.

A light poked through the snow. It moved toward him, sweeping its white beam from left to right, as though feeling its way in the darkness. Vernon stared. He looked at his watch, 2:40 a.m. The first arrival was not due for at least a half-hour. The beam continued to search, moving closer. The outline of an aircraft appeared, a large airplane, a taildragger. The green and white beacon from the tower flashed overhead, and the deep rumble of radial engines vibrated the windows. All the company aircraft were turbines. Nobody used radial engines around there. Other companies still used DC-3s, but none came there. He watched the light, thick in the blowing snow. The airplane took shape, a twin engine with two rudders—an old Twin Beech. The radial engines sent a deep throb into Vernon's insides. He remembered the same twins hauling passengers out of that very terminal forty years earlier.

The twin swiveled around, blowing snow in a great cloud toward the glass. Vernon left his office, ran down the hallway, and through the door. Once in the snow he moved quickly toward the airplane. Snow blew in cold eddies around him. He wore no coat, but ignored the cold. He carried the logbook.

"Peggy, remember the Twin Beech we took to Florida?" His voice was happy. He started to run and slipped, recovered and continued. The green and white lights washed above. The Twin Beech shut one engine down, and a cargo door swung open. A vague face looked out from the darkened fuselage.

"Hello!" Vernon called. No one answered. "Have you come for me?" He stopped in front of the open door. The face leaned out.

"What?" It was a young face on a young man dressed in blue jeans and a nylon parka. He needed a shave and chewed gum nervously.

"Did you come for me?" Vernon asked again, feeling something was wrong.

"You from FedEx?" the pilot asked and kicked at the doorframe to keep his feet warm. "I've never flown in here; normally go into Cedar Rapids, but it's closed. There's supposed to be a truck meet me here. You it?"

Vernon shook his head slowly and stared at the airplane. The one radial still running ticked evenly.

"If you're not it, I'm closing the door. It's cold out here. Where's your coat?" the pilot asked.

Vernon suddenly felt the cold. "I... What year is this?" he asked. The pilot was already reaching for the door. "This? Ah, I think it's a '48, '47 or a '48. Hell, I don't know."

"No, I mean what year is it now?"

The pilot tilted his head. "Look, I think you'd better get inside or get home. You can't be standing around in the cold like that. Why don't you go in? The van's pulling up now."

Vernon turned. A large van pulled through the gate and past his car still perched on the snow bank. He walked back to the terminal, his elbow beginning to ache again. Before he reached the door, he turned. "Is your name, Dansig?" he called. "Charles S. Dansig?"

The pilot shook his head and waved the delivery van back toward the airplane.

Vernon walked along the hallway and returned his office. He sat. Emotion drained from him, leaving only an emptiness. The Twin Beech fired its other engine and Vernon listened to it taxi away and, then, silence. He sat, unmoving. He felt foolish. He glanced at the photographs.

"Ghosts," he said. "I wanted ghosts." Planting his elbows on the desk, he rubbed his face with both hands. A white light flashed through the window moving his shadow momentarily across the wall where the photographs had been. He glanced over his shoulder. The control tower's beam pulsated once, white, and then seconds later, white again, no green. He barely noted it. Another airplane taxied toward the terminal, its light searching through the snow. A large piston engine shook the windows again. Vernon chuckled. "Not one of mine," he said.

He kept his back to the window. The airplane's landing light poked through the glass again, keeping Vernon's shadow on the wall. He held his head in his hands. The engine ticked at idle behind him, and a strong wind shook the building. He glanced up. The flicker of the fluorescent bulb was the only movement in the hallway, but he felt something.

"Baloney," he said, still leaning on the desk. But something was moving, moving toward him. He listened and heard nothing other than the snow against glass and the airplane's motor outside. His shadow barely moved beside the doorframe. The hallway light flickered. Suddenly, someone appeared in the doorway, filling the frame.

"You have something of mine," a deep voice said. He stood in shadow, the light from outside not reaching him. Vernon sat frozen, his shadow unmoving. The figure raised an arm into the light. It was coated in thick leather, its hand in heavy gauntlet. A finger pointed toward him. "There, on the desk."

Vernon barely moved his eyes, looking where the figure indicated. The logbook.

"No need to be surprised," the voice said, now almost friendly. "You've been looking for me. I felt it, so I came."

Vernon spoke, his voice a thin creak. "Dansig? Charles S. Dansig?"

"Charlie. I need the logbook. I never filled in my last flight, you know." His hand opened slowly.

Vernon picked the book from the desk and started to hand it to him. "I...I suspected there might be...things...like you." The hand still reached out waiting for the book. "Are there others?"

"Yes."

Vernon glanced at the wedding photo, the Navy photo. "All the others?"

"Somewhere."

"Do you know them?"

"Some."

"Can you...can I...?"

"I cannot, but you can."

"How?"

"You found me, didn't you?"

"Yes, but...."

"Find them." With that, the figure stretched its hand even further. "Please, I must go."

Vernon looked outside at the airplane, a biplane, a Boeing Model 40, airmail. A steady white beacon light flashed—no green. He remembered the old airway beacons flashing solid white when he was a kid. He looked back at the figure, still in shadow. He stood and moved closer. The nearer he got, the vaguer the figure became. He could almost see through it to the hallway.

"Please," the voice said.

Vernon placed the logbook in the outstretched hand. The fingers closed, and the figure vanished almost instantly along the hallway toward the flickering light. Vernon ran to the window. The solid white beacon flashed, and the Boeing 40, under a blast of power swiveled its tail and disappeared in a cloud of twisting snow. The beacon from the tower flashed white...then green. Vernon sat lightly at the desk and picked up the wedding photograph. A lightness overcame him, and he ran his fingers over Peggy's face.

"Just find them," he said. "Find them."

"Just Another Hangar"

Part I

Crossing over the field I saw it. A small airport like so many others in the Midwest, it had one runway and one large hangar. It wasn't on the chart, but I didn't see any X's on the runway to indicate it was closed, and the worst that could happen would be I'd be told to get lost. Throughout my first summer as a gypsy pilot I'd been told to get lost before, so....

I circled the north-south strip and noted that the wind was out of the northwest at about 15 knots. The air was warm coming through the Aeronca Champ's side window. Below, the corn was deep green with gold tassels. The fields moved in the wind like ocean waves eliminating the need for a windsock. With a good cornfield you can see the wind, all of it, and judge how it will snuggle the aircraft right to the ground.

Turning downwind I closed the throttle, and the 65-horse engine popped once. I continued in a left bank to base leg and then onto final, watching the corn while picking my spot on the sod runway. A quick glance at the tattered windsock confirmed what the corn had already told me. I felt smug, the worst feeling a pilot can get, because it means you don't know nuthin' and might be too stupid to learn. At 19 I hadn't learned how to learn yet, too stupid to know how dumb I was.

With left wing down, I flew low across the fence and rolled the left wheel onto the grass. Slight forward pressure on the stick kept the Champ planted on the ground as the tail eased itself down and airspeed bled off. The smell of warm earth flowed through the open window.

A pair of yellow-painted tires marked where to taxi off the runway without dropping into the drainage ditch along the edge. It was an unpretentious airport with only the one building and no fuel pumps. I taxied behind the hangar out of the wind and turning hard, swung the tail over a tie-down rope. Two more ropes were under the wings in the weeds. I reached behind to snap off the magnetos. The propeller took one easy swing and stopped.

The ropes under the wings proved little more than weathered stumps of hemp, so I grabbed my own from the baggage compartment where I kept my sleeping bag, dirty laundry, tools and a half-dozen Snickers Bars. While threading the ropes through the rusty eyehooks in the dirt I stared at the hangar. Its wood had weathered gray long ago. About two stories high, I guessed it covered two, maybe three thousand square feet, at any rate, too large for such a small airfield.

The hangar's two immense door halves shook and complained with each gust of wind much as a ship would at dock in choppy waters. Either that or that something was inside trying to huff its way out.

Sparrows darted through the many cracks. A strip of corrugated steel trim flapped above the door track. I pictured it ripping off to fly through the air and slice through my fabric wing, or me. But I realized it had survived untold years without falling so I ignored it. I'd learned long ago to ignore whatever threatened or I couldn't understand.

I walked through the dry weeds to the far side of the hangar where parked outside were two abandoned Navions and a Luscombe fuselage discarded on its side in the dirt. Navions were once sleek low-wing four-seaters, built, it was dreamed, for returning P-51 pilots. And before the war that had created the Mustang heroes, the Luscombe had been a quick two-seat tail dragger, a delight to fly. Now, in 1986, they were abandoned hulks.

A small greasy dog lay beneath the Navion's wing. He lifted his head, gave a disinterested bark as I neared and was back asleep before I could answer. He didn't seem to believe I was there, or care.

The two Navions were identical. Both sat on flat tires, and their once orange paint schemes had faded to a dull yellow like old banana custard that no one wanted. One airplane's nose strut was extended to its limit leaving the tail low. It had no propeller, and a glance under the cowling showed all the cylinders gone leaving only empty holes in the case. Rusty connecting rods poked out. I started to reach inside when a pair of wasps flew past squelching that idea.

Breaching all forms of airport etiquette I climbed onto a wing and the Navion moaned under my weight.

"Sorry," I said. "I'll only be a minute; just want to look inside, into your past."

Little was visible through the cracked and frosted Plexiglas. I tried the canopy, and it complained but gave. Time and unknown grave robbers had ravaged the interior and cannibalized the instrument panel. The upholstery was faded, torn, and the carpet pulled up revealing corroded aluminum. Everything was coated with bits of hay, cornstalk and age.

I found the registration pouch on the pilot's side, but the documents inside were little more than yellowed scraps. One form, though, was preserved well enough to read the owner's name— Emilio Nervino.

"Well, Mr. Nervino," I said to the form, "I hope you don't mind me poking around your airplane." A sharp screech flashed by my ear. Wasps, I thought and jumped back dropping the document pouch.

A sparrow perched on the canopy lip and scolded me. She beat her wings like an enraged nun to emphasize her point, whatever it was, and with a final annoyed chirp flew off.

I picked the registration pouch from the seat, slid it back in place and closed the canopy. When I climbed down the Navion moaned relief, waking the greasy dog that now followed me to the hangar.

Despite the airport's state of advanced decay a freshly painted metal sign reading, LEARN TO FLY, hung above a single door. A wind gust shook the building, which appeared ready to blow away with the next blast. The new sign, however, was anchored firmly to the wall, amazingly out of place, its message more of a taunt than an invitation to me.

"Wanna go inside, boy?" I called to the dog now leaning against the door. I expected him to bounce off the ground, tail wagging in appreciation, but he hardly raised his head long enough to cast a disapproving gaze. I felt silly. Dogs have that effect on me.

"Well, suit yourself," I said and opened the door. The dog slipped quietly inside, and the door closed behind us.

It was cool like the inside of a cave, or a tomb I thought and was content with that metaphor until I realized I'd never been inside a tomb or a cave for that matter. My eyes took several minutes adjusting to the dim light and knowing I would stumble over the dog if I moved, I stood and listened.

The wind sang through the high ceiling where sparrows flew between the rafters.

Gradually my eyes adjusted to the dark. The hangar was crowded with a lifetime's worth of aviation stuff. Nearest me was a Globe Swift—a low wing, two-seat monoplane, silver with blue trim and a tinted canopy. Its nose bowl grill smiled at me the way I imagined a crocodile might smile at a poodle. It had one gear leg extended under a wing and the other wing was supported by a jack stand. It sat as if waiting for something. A wheel sat nearby on an upturned crate. The dust on each piece gave the impression that someone had been repairing the landing gear, decided to step out for a beer and disappeared into the far stretches of the Universe. I've known beer to have that effect.

Behind the Swift was a Champ like mine, except orange and yellow in the original paint scheme with the orange sweeping under its belly. The fabric was cracked and brittle, looking as if it would punch through with the slightest pressure. A sweater was draped across the front seat and hanging on the joystick was an olive green baseball cap—the old kind without the plastic adjusting band on the back. Like the Swift, this airplane seemed hastily abandoned some years before.

Scattered around the hangar were engines and parts of engines. Magnetos on benches, a carburetor shared a moldy wooden box with a mouse nest. Spare doors, one I recognized from a Fairchild 24, hung along one wall. A four-cylinder Franklin engine was on the floor against a parts washing tank. A large radial sat on a pallet beside the Champ, a crated propeller beside it. Suspended from the walls were wings—some with fabric, and others stripped bare, ribs exposed.

Workbenches and tool chests on wheels stood curiously undisturbed throughout the hangar. Two red barrels, one labeled, 40W and the other, 50W, rested on stands near a small door labeled, MEN'S, and what appeared as an afterthought, AND WOMEN'S, TOO—KNOCK FIRST.

Suddenly, birds chirped wildly above me in the rafters, fighting over some contested piece of territory or a particular female's attention. The racket subsided with the loser winging across the room and landing on the propeller tip of a Cessna 195.

Then, I saw someone move.

The figure moved quickly around the propeller and disappeared again into the shadows. He made no noise. With the dog following, I picked my way carefully around the Cessna's tail toward the far corner of the hangar and found him standing on the opposite side of a Ryan PT-22 monoplane. Only his legs showed beneath the Kinner radial engine. I remained fixed in shadow just the other side of the Ryan. I made no sound, nor did the dog.

A row of small windows along the ceiling at this end of the hangar let in enough light for me to see that the Ryan was a seemingly functional airplane, the first I'd seen since landing. Gradually, I maneuvered myself around its tail until I could see him from the side and slightly behind. He seemed not to notice me, being absorbed with something in the engine.

I guessed him to be in his late fifties, maybe six feet tall, dark and stocky with a thick neck and closely trimmed gray hair. He wore stiff white overalls with LEARN TO FLY stenciled across the back. With one arm he reached far behind the engine while the other arm arched over a cylinder head. The two hands tried to meet somewhere in a tight corner near the firewall.

"Come on, you piece of...there. Gotchya!" The dark figure swiveled his head like a mud turtle and looked at a toolbox just out of reach to his left. I stood quietly behind to his right.

End Part I

Part II

From Part I: I guessed him to be in his late fifties, maybe six feet tall, dark and stocky with a thick neck and closely trimmed gray hair. He wore stiff white overalls with LEARN TO FLY stenciled across the back. With one arm he reached far behind the engine while the other arm arched over a cylinder head. The two hands tried to meet somewhere in a tight corner near the firewall.

"Come on, you piece of...there. Gotchya!" The dark figure swiveled his head like a mud turtle and looked at a toolbox just out of reach to his left. I stood quietly behind to his right.

"Hand me those wire cutters, will ya," he called and waved toward the toolbox without looking at me. "Those, next to the safety wire. I don't want to let go of this thing; took me forever to reach it...gotta get me a pair of wire twisters someday."

The dog sat beside the toolbox and gave me a look of, "Well, are you going to get the wire cutters or what?"

"These the ones?" I asked picking out a large pair.

"No, the smaller ones...yeah, those, thanks." He took them from me, and with much face making and grunting completed whatever it was he was after.

"Why-the-hell is everything you want to work on always where you can't reach it?" he asked without waiting for my answer.

His accent was out of place for the Midwest, more like East Coast, New York or Philadelphia. He tended to run words together and squash his r's, so "wire cutters" became, "wiyah cuttahs." But he spoke inconsistently, the accent appearing briefly throughout the more commonplace flat Midwest tone.

I expected him to ask what I was doing there or tell me his name while offering his hand. Instead, he pulled an oily rag from his back pocket and disappeared around to the other side of the Ryan while wiping his hands.

"What's that dog doing in here?" he asked. The dog was lying on the cool slab of concrete near the tail wheel. "He's supposed to stay outside," he snapped again while reaching down to scratch the dog's head. "Keeps messin' the place up." He stood and took a small bowl from the workbench, upsetting a coffee can full of nuts and screws in the process. They scattered across the bench and onto the floor, bouncing and skipping under tables and into dark corners.

"Stupid dog. I told you he messes the place up."

He filled the dish with water and placed it on the floor near the dog, who ignored it, and then gathered most of the hardware and put it on the bench.

"Name's Nervino; Emilio Nervino. Some call me Ed." He flashed a wide grin showing a perfect row of white teeth. "What do some call you?"

"I just flew in..." I said.

"That tells me what you did, not who you are."

"Oh, I saw your hangar from above and it looked like a pretty good place to..."

"Now I'm finding out why you're here; still don't know who you are. You got a name?"

"Yes..."

"Good. Hand me that grease gun near the phone."

He pointed to a table behind me in an exceptionally dark section of the hangar. The grease gun sat wrapped in a rag below a plate on the wall where a phone had once hung. Beside the plate was an old calendar with a picture of Santa Claus in flying goggles and leather helmet sitting astride an Archer Aero oil can rocketing across a starry night sky. A fiery plume trailed behind and Santa waved merrily at the viewer. The date on the calendar: December 1960.

Its proximity to the missing phone had once made the calendar an ideal message pad with names and phone numbers scrawled across the page and onto the wall. I read:

DECEMBER 1—PICK UP DALE AT CSQ

DECEMBER 3—JIM, 9 AM; DON, 11 AM; KATE, 3 PM

DECEMBER 6—OFF

And on it went.

Greasy fingerprints smeared the notes. I wondered if any of the people attached to those names were still in the area or even alive, for that matter. I wanted to call them later on the off chance that one might be at the old number. But then, what would I say if they did answer?

"Ah, hello. You don't know me, but I got your name off a hangar wall, and I was just wondering if you were still alive, still flying..."

Ed interrupted. "You found that grease gun yet?"

"Got it now." I grabbed the gun and left the rag behind, instantly getting grease all over my hands.

"Let's have it here." He took the gun and moved around the airplane lubricating things I never knew needed grease. Finished, he tossed the gun onto the bench and hit the coffee can with the screws. Again, hardware bounced on the floor. Several pieces dropped into the dog's water. Ed ignored it this time and unlatched the hangar's double doors.

"Get the other door, will ya," he called. "There're two pins in the floor; you need to pull them up, then unhook the door near the handle. The whole thing slides open after that."

He slid his half of the old doors open while I pulled the pins, unfastened the hook and tried to push mine. It was heavy and barely moved. Ed's half slammed against the stops, and he turned to charge mine. It groaned and slid onto the outriggers. The wind, calmer now, gently rocked the open doors. Sparrows flew out the door startled by the sudden wave of sunlight that poured over the Ryan. Its white wings and tail feathers shone in the glare. The green fuselage had none of the chalky white stains that soiled everything else in the hangar.

"Whose Champ is that?" Ed called.

"I'll move it." I answered and ran toward my airplane.

"Still doesn't tell me whose it is," he mumbled. "No need to move it, fine where it is." He rummaged through the small baggage compartment in the Ryan's fuselage, removed two leather helmets with goggles and dropped them on a wing.

In full daylight the Ryan was an absolute beauty. There were no traces of the oil and exhaust stains normally present on aircraft its age. The monoplane was spotless as though wiped clean after each flight.

"Does this thing ever fly?" I asked thinking he might have recently rebuilt it.

"Fly it all the time," he said. "Grab a wing."

I took the handhold on the left wing, and we moved the Ryan out of the hangar tail first. We rotated it until it pointed toward the runway.

"Ever prop one of these?" he called from the wing root as he loosened parachute straps on the front seat.

"Yes," I lied.

"It's not like that Champ of yours, you know." He knew I lied. "Go ahead, pull it through a couple of times; I'll tell you when to stop." He swung himself into the rear cockpit.

I hesitated staring at the long wooden prop.

"Switch is OFF."

One prop tip pointed toward seven o'clock, so I didn't have far to reach. After I had pulled it through about six times he called, "There, that should be a good spot. Switch is ON. Brakes are probably on, too."

I took hold of the propeller blade again and gave a reasonable heave while walking it through to my right. It left my hand before I had time to realize. The Kinner barked dully, coughed and barked again, before setting up its distinct, pok-pok—apok-apok rhythm. Ed grinned from the rear cockpit while waving me into the front.

The prop blast slapped my pants legs as I stood on the wing pushing aside the parachute straps on the seat. Right foot over the rim, then left, then I banged my shins before I lowered myself in. Buckles and straps slipped and clanked against the metal fuselage. Finally strapped in, I donned the helmet he'd set on the joystick for me. Immediately, his voice came hollow through the Gosport tube attached to the earflaps.

"You in okay?"

"Yeah," I yelled into a plastic funnel hanging near my knee. I assumed this was the speaking portion of the primitive intercom. It was either that or I had just yelled into a relief tube.

"Good," he came back assuaging my concerns. The joystick swung a wide circle and banged against my knees, Ed's way of showing how much room he'd need. The throttle inched forward, and the Kinner's cylinders in front of me shuddered. The fuel gauge bounced in its glass tube over the nose tank. The engine gave a clacking belch and the propeller blew dust and weeds into my Champ tied behind.

Ed wasted no time on a run-up. He taxied onto the runway, pointed the nose into the wind and pushed the throttle and stick forward. Barely had we started to roll when the tail lifted and the pok-pokking mass of 1940s Ryan climbed into the Midwestern sky.

The left wing dropped, and we passed across the corn without climbing. I pictured the knuckled landing gear hanging like a wasp's legs as we flew across fields, rising casually over hedge trees, corncribs and Aeromotor windmills.

Over a bean field, he lifted the nose and opened the throttle. The engine shook as Ed made a slow spiral climb banking first to the left and then to the right. Somewhere about 1500 feet above the ground he leveled. I glanced over my shoulder and saw his eyes smile through the goggles. Put a pair of machine-guns in front of him and he could have been straight out of Dawn Patrol.

He inscribed a circle with his left hand in the air. I gathered we would soon be out of straight and level. I nodded. I reached to tighten my straps when the stick shot forward, throttle back, and the nose dropped. I grasped the cockpit's rim. Airspeed rose; wind rushed through the wires and cylinder cooling fins. The stick came back, nose up, throttle forward, engine banging, and the horizon dropped. Blue sky, blue sky, more sky, speed bleeding off; over the top, and I looked straight up into cornfields. The nose came over dropping down from the top of the loop. The throttle well back producing that gentle pok, pok, pok of the Kinner, and the corn slid beneath us in a blur.

Before I could digest this, the nose came up again with the throttle less than full. The stick shot back abruptly, and a heavy dose of rudder sent us plowing into a heavy snap roll to the left. We rolled level, the nose dipped slightly for speed, then again the stick came back as Ed stomped the right rudder snapping us the opposite way. The Kinner radial engine that normally took two adults to lift onto its mounts, twisted effortlessly through the afternoon sky. Its black cylinders never complained. We turned wide to the left, back toward the airport.

He leveled the wings and let the nose drop to gain speed. Then up it came, throttle wide open, and the stick, this time, moved forward as we approached vertical. Ed kicked the tail out from under us with a heavy foot on the rudder. The old Ryan arched over onto its wing, almost hovering in the sky for a moment and then gravity sucked us straight down toward the fields below. From the corner of my vision I could see the flying wires flex and bow under the strain.

We leveled. Ed rocked the wings from side to side. The hot August sun hammered on my leather helmet. Despite the open cockpit I was sweating heavily, wrung out. I poked my face into the slipstream and watched the ground slide beneath. The wind grabbed my cheeks trying to pull my skin off.

"You'll get bugs in your teeth doin' that," came the voice through the Gosport. I wanted to tell him I'd had enough but was embarrassed to admit it. I wondered how much more I could take before I really embarrassed myself by adding an unwanted stripe down one side of the fuselage. Somehow, he sensed my thoughts, and a thick calm settled over the entire airplane. My uneasiness faded, and we flew across Iowa in no particular direction.

I knew so little about this person, Emilio "Ed" Nervino. I had walked into his hangar an uninvited stranger and now found myself soaking up his unique brand of hospitality.

The left wing dipped, its round tip pointed toward a herd of cattle eating their way across a pasture. The wing rose again and stopped on a distant puff of cloud, the only relief in the sky.

I watched the summer scene, flat and hot, skim past us. We were two creatures from the Earth, completely without feathers, heads peeping out of a machine from an era long faded. We were headed nowhere and would arrive only when it was right. Ed flew with the ease of someone having spent a lifetime in the sky. There was no faking this talent. This was not by-the-book aviation. This was flight, pure and honest. He said nothing at this point. The great wealth of his experience, the years of oil-spitting engines and countless miles of sky could not be confined to the rear cockpit. It overflowed onto the fuselage, along the wings and enveloped me.

The warm sun must have lulled me into forgetting time when Ed's voice came through the tube: "I have to be getting you back now."

I shuddered. A cold blast of wind slipped over my damp back. The day was still warm, and evening a long way off.

We dragged low across the cornfield, over the wire fence, and the Ryan squatted onto the runway. The windsock atop the hangar flicked listlessly while Ed taxied back, s-turning to see where he was headed. I removed my helmet and felt the soft air flow across my scalp. The world spun past when the tail dragger pivoted on one wheel until it was pointed back into the hangar. He switched the magnetos off, and the Kinner rattled to a stop. The propeller took a few easy swings before it was still. I sat for a long moment feeling too relaxed to climb out.

I fly. I know that world up there—a world open exclusively to those who want it; those not interested should remain on the ground, no hard feelings, but it's your loss. Ed had shown me that same world from his viewpoint, from his machine, in his way. With perfect understanding of his corner of that world, he shared the vision with a stranger. It took little effort, but the impact left me seated in the Ryan's front cockpit wanting to know more about him.

He'd climbed down and stood by the left wing. He smiled. I felt as though he saw straight into my thoughts, an unfair advantage since I couldn't see back. There was a strong urge to speak, to question and toss out defenses against this intrusion. The feeling dissipated when he slapped the wing's fabric and said, "Hop down and grab your wing, get this rag bucket inside."

The Ryan rolled smoothly into the hangar and came to rest against the chocks where it had been parked before. The hangar door halves, however, were less cooperative and stuck just short of closing.

"Push from the outside," he said.

I stepped through the crack between the two doors and grabbed a handle. We both pushed, and it closed with a deep-throated, BONG, echoing through the building. I stood outside for a moment staring at the closed hangar doors.

"I'll go around through the other door," I called but heard no reply, only the scraping of the latch being bolted from inside.

The wind had increased again, and scraps of dried weeds swirled around my feet as I made my way to the far side of the hangar. A cloud of dust blew against the door below the LEARN TO FLY sign. I reached for the handle and pulled. The door lurched but did not open. I jiggled the handle and still nothing—locked.

"Mmmm," I murmured and looked through the glass. The Swift and the Cessna were both visible, but nothing inside moved. There was no sign of Ed. Confused, I glanced to either side looking for a second door I might have overlooked. But this was the only door on this side, and it was unmistakably locked.

I knocked while peering through the glass. Only the occasional sparrow moved inside. The wind shook the building, and the LEARN TO FLY sign banged against the wall over my head.

"There's no one there."

I turned quickly and saw a woman astride a horse near the corner of the hangar.

"What...?"

"There's no one there," she repeated. "You're wasting your time." She spoke with cool self-assurance and pulled the horse's head sharply with the reins to keep it from sampling the weeds.

Amid the rotted Navions and tired hangar she was out of place atop the bay mare dressed in hacking coat and boots. Her glossy blonde hair streaked with silver was tucked snug into a bun welded to the back of her head. The horse stepped restlessly to the side and was corrected with a jerk of the reins without her looking at the animal.

"I know someone's here," I said. "I just landed."

"Yes." She interrupted. "I saw you come in. We keep the runway open all year round, but there really is nothing here."

"Who's we?" I became annoyed with this woman on her horse.

"We, the Nervinos. We own all this." She gestured with her crop. "I'm Kate Nervino. My Uncle Ed once ran a flying business out here."

"Once?"

"He was fairly wealthy, although certainly not from flying. Owned several businesses in New York at one time but left all that to move out here. Anyhow, this was his. He gave flying lessons, fixed old airplanes..."

"Your uncle—Ed...Emilio Nervino?"

"Yes. Emilio." She laughed. "No one called him that."

"What...? Did he go broke or something?" I was confused.

"Oh, no." She paused and then, "He died. Apparently he had high blood pressure, or something, and the government said he was grounded. I was just a girl at the time." Her voice softened. "He used to take me flying. He was a beautiful man, a very good pilot; lived for flying. He was forever taking strangers up for rides or fixing their airplanes without charging. No way to run a business.

"Anyway," she continued, "when the FAA told him he couldn't fly anymore, he just closed up shop one day, went home, and gradually rotted away until he died several months later." Her voice was distant and cold. "He lost interest."

"When did this happen?" My voice was hollow, as if the words had come from someone else's mouth.

"Well, he lost his medical in December of Nineteen, ah...Sixty. I remember I was out here for Christmas. And he died in early spring, just when the air was turning warm."

A gust of wind shook the hangar violently and rattled the LEARN TO FLY sign. The sign, fresh paint gone, was old and faded by weather and years, and the wind threatened to carry it away.

"In his will, he stipulated the runway be kept open to anyone wanting to use it. The hangar was to be left untouched." She gazed at the decaying structure. "Nobody's been in there since he died."

The wind felt cold.

"You're welcome to use the airport," she called and turned the horse's head. "But there's really nothing here." She trotted off along a dirt road toward a grove of cottonwoods.

I ran around the hangar looking for an entrance, but none existed except a small window at eye level on the west wall. Through it I could see the Ryan exactly where we'd put it moments before. The light was enough to make out details but not strong enough to explain them away.

The Ryan's tires were flat and cracked. The wings, previously white and glistening, were now covered in grime. The airplane had aged decades in the time it had taken to leave Ed and get to this window. The fabric was pockmarked with small holes from mice or fallen debris. The fuselage, once polished green, was now dull and covered with white bird crap. An abandoned nest was wedged between two engine cylinders.

On the workbench below the windowsill were Ed's overalls covered in the greasy dust of time. Mice had eaten a large hole through the lettering on the back, through the LEARN TO FLY.

The wind was stiff when I taxied away from the hangar in the Champ. Before taking off, I saw the greasy dog walk slowly toward the Navions. He stopped under the wing where I had found him earlier, pawed the ground without interest and settled down. His gaze caught mine briefly before his head dropped, eyes closed in sleep, and I left. My gypsy summer could now change into autumn and I could begin to learn to fly.

©1986

"The Last Ride Forever"

She stepped carefully over the top strand of the wire fence. A rusty barb tore at her dressing gown, refusing to let her proceed. With one hand on the old dry post, Eva clutched the gown and pulled.

The cotton skirt ripped in a long, ragged strip from her knee to across her hip. She wanted to cry. The wind, although light, was warm and carried forgotten smells from the pinewoods across the abandoned runway.

Everything was exactly as it had once been, but everything had changed.

Weeds obscured the ramp where once a dozen small airplanes had parked. The pole where the SHELL fuel sign had been was still visible. Even the ring where the enamel yellow sign hung still remained, only now it looked to Eva like a basketball hoop set the wrong way. A sparrow perched in the center, its head twitching in the breeze, ignoring her. She clutched the tattered gown as best she could around her thin legs and set out across the field.

Overhead, the whine of an airliner slowly crossed the sky. She watched the jet lower its wheels on final approach to the international airport only three miles away. The sun glinted off the jet's fuselage, and it rocked briefly in the wind. When she turned her eyes back to the old airstrip, the sparrow was gone.

She wanted to stop. Her breath came hard, her heart pounding in her temples and ears, her vision suddenly cloudy. The climb over the barbed wire fence had somehow exhausted her. Eva desperately wanted to get across the runway to the parking ramp, to the old building just visible against the pine trees.

"Should have worn my shoes," she mumbled looking at her bare feet in the dry weeds. The torn hospital gown did little to block the wind, but she could not remember why she was wearing it.

Another jet descended across the trees, its landing gear popping out at the same spot where the last one had extended its.

"Like robots," Eva said with a smile. "Can't think for themselves."

The runway was almost completely overgrown with stubby vegetation. The black hardtop had decomposed into gray pebbles laced with cracks where the weeds had taken root. Slowly the old pavement was returning to earth. When the weeds had broken the pavement into small enough pieces, the pine trees would take root, and eventually there would be no trace of the airfield ever having been there. Eva took all this in without sadness. She was resigned to the strip's fate, almost happy.

The gravel crunched under her bare feet in soft contrast to the stream of jets overhead. A flight of robins, headed north, popped from the trees and swooped low over her head. Friendly chirps blended perfectly with her footsteps.

"Doris and George ran the Taylorcraft off the runway right over there," she said and pointed toward a dusty pit beneath a line of scrub oak. She laughed. "Doris said George was flying, and George swore he told her to make the landing…" She stopped and put a thin white hand to her chin, the delicate fingertips touching her dry lips. She tilted her head, seeing what was long gone. "I think Doris was paying more attention to George, than the airplane, and I know George had his eyes on other things than the runway." She stared at the empty pit beside the runway, the only thing there, now, a dozen empty beer cans and a shopping cart turned on its side.

Eva walked down the abandoned runway and stared at the chain link fence that cut across it two thirds of the way down. The city had years before converted the land into a parking area for its road equipment, and erected a fence across the runway around a collection of snow plows. She looked beyond the fence.

What drew her along was the hangar, or what was left of it, at the far end of the field. It was the only structure remaining.

"I soloed here," she announced to no one. "In April, April the 16th, 1940." She stepped on a stone and recoiled, almost falling. Her strength was failing rapidly, her vision was fading, she longed to sleep, to lie on the broken pavement amid the tall weeds and sleep.

"I soloed here," she repeated. "In a Waco. That's a biplane, an awfully big biplane." She listened to more robins flying out from the trees; their voices as sweet as the spring air itself, their energy as young and vital, as she felt old and wasted. She looked down at the white hospital gown, and a shudder of fear raced through her. She gathered the skirt tight around her and headed toward the hangar.

"Yes," she cried, "I soloed here." Her feet scraped on the old pavement, her steps quickening. "I made three landings—good landings. Although, maybe, I bounced the first one just a little." Tears rose to her eyes, further clouding her vision. She hurried toward the hangar so far away. "I remember that big radial engine swinging a massive silver propeller. I was so scared of that when I first flew, but after eight or ten hours I came to love it."

She left the runway for the taller weeds along the chain link fence. Her fingers clutched at the metal weave, and she pulled herself along, hand over hand, her breath coming in short tight spasms as she tried to reach the hangar.

"There were so many of us!" she cried aloud. "So many, and everyone so young and beautiful and so...so..." She leaned her face against the chain mail, her voice coming in sobs. "Jack took the Cub up one afternoon and did twenty loops in a row. Beth, took that as a challenge, and as soon as he landed, hopped in and did twenty-five." She pushed away from the fence and ran her fingers through the few strands of gray hair left on her head. "Then Allison showed them all up by doing thirty loops and a five-turn spin back into the pattern."

The pine trees moaned with the wind. Eva drew closer to the hangar. Its boards weathered gray, its windows either missing entirely or cracked. She stepped past a rusted twist of steel tubing with a small tree growing through it. It was a fuselage, but from what she could only guess. A chipmunk sat on the highest point, its front paws held as though in prayer, its eyes fixed and staring. Below him, the grass moved where a snake gradually wound its way along a tube, coiling up towards the chipmunk.

Eva stared. The chipmunk remained immobile, the snake inching ever closer. The wind blew the aroma of the warm pines toward them, and she saw the snake's tongue shoot out, probing. She wanted to shout, to warn the little animal, but her voice failed her. Gradually, the snake worked his way through the remains of the old airplane, reaching for the chipmunk.

Eva turned to the hangar. She could see where the flying school's sign had once hung. The COCA COLA sign was still there, but it was shot full of rusty holes, so only the tip of the green bottle was still recognizable.

She looked back at the chipmunk. It never moved.

'Run!' she wanted to shout, but the sound never left her voice. The snake, its tongue shooting forth in quick stabs, moved closer.

"Ed was a flight instructor here," she said, purposefully turning away from the snake. "That's where I met him." She pointed at the hangar, to a small door beside the riddled COCA COLA sign. "That was the office. It was full of model airplanes suspended from the ceiling by strings, so whenever anyone opened the door all the little airplanes would dance around like they were caught in a storm."

She smiled.

She glanced at the chipmunk, still motionless on the fuselage, its paws still in prayer. The snake was now only inches below him.

"There was a map on the wall, too," she said too loudly. "A map of the whole country, with a tack marking this airport, and a string off that so you could measure distances to any place else in the country."

The snake was now within striking distance of the chipmunk, but still it refused to move, or admit to the danger.

'Why don't you do something?' she screamed, but again, the voice only echoed in her head, never reaching the animal.

Slowly, the snake's head rose.

"Do something!"

"We're doing something," the young man's voice came softly through the fog. "You just relax."

Eva's vision broke through a heavy cloud. She was no longer at the airport, no longer staring at the hangar and the snake.

"What?" she asked, confused, and saw the doctor leaning over her bed, one hand on her shoulder the other holding a chart in a gray metal folder.

"Can you hear me, Mrs. Gwyer?" He shouted the question, as though calling to her down a long tunnel. She heard his voice, but wanted to ignore him. She turned her head on the pillow and looked down at her feet. The blankets were pulled back, and a nurse rubbed lotion onto her frail twig legs. The hospital gown was bunched to one side.

"I'll give you something to help you sleep," the young doctor shouted again and wrote furiously in the metal folder before snapping it shut. She only caught his eyes once, deep set and dark—tired and impersonal eyes.

"I want..." Eva said and forgot what she wanted.

"What, Dear," the nurse's friendly voice asked. "What do you want?"

Eva strained to remember what she wanted. She knew she had been dreaming, but the dream was vanishing until all she could remember was the snake.

"A snake," she announced. 'No, that can't be right,' she thought and laughed inside her head.

"You want a snake?" the nurse asked with an amused lilt in her voice. "I don't think you want that. Now, just let me turn you over and I'll get your back."

Eva felt herself being gently rolled over. She felt as though her body was a light bag of fragile bones ready to crack. Her face pressed into the pillow, her nose filled with the sanitized odor of hospital linen. Across the room she recognized a face, her daughter.

The woman, in her mid-40s, stood alone and sad in the shadows, staring at her dying mother being rubbed and charted by the staff. Eva smiled and saw her daughter force a smile in return.   'Why is she so gloomy?' she asked herself, feeling her senses sharpen. "Barbara?" she called.

"Yes, Mom," her daughter answered and moved toward the bed.

"What am I doing here?" she asked. Her daughter started to answer and looked to the doctor, who shrugged, not an I-don't-know shrug but more I-can't-help. Eva tapped her almost hairless skull weakly. "I feel something going on in here, Barbara. There's something taking me away...."

She closed her eyes.

The doctor took Barbara aside. "She's in little pain," he said. He spoke mechanically, having been on duty for over twenty-three hours already. "She'll talk about strange things; brain tumors do that. One minute lucid; the next she could babble like an infant."

"How much longer?"

"Anytime," he said. "All we can do is keep her comfortable."

"What, no more miracle cures like the chemotherapy, until the rest of her hair falls out? Or maybe teeth or eyes?"

"I'm sorry. We had to try, but we can't always..."

She cut him off with a wave, and he left the room. The nurse finished the rubdown, rolled Eva onto her back and tucked the blankets securely around her. She then placed the oxygen tubes back into her nostrils and started to leave.

"Thank-you," Barbara said, her voice hollow.

"Your mother has been talking about airplanes a great deal. Did she work for the airlines?"

Barbara thought for a minute. "No," she said. And then, "But she was a pilot..."

"Oh?"

"A long time ago, before the war, before I was born. And during the war she flew with the WASP...."

"Oh, I've heard of them," the nurse said and tried to recall the acronym: "Women's Air Something Planes?"

"Women Airforce Service Pilots...yes. She flew bombers on, ah, ferry flights, during the war."

"Really?" The nurse seemed honestly impressed.

Barbara laughed. "I haven't thought about that in years; she rarely ever mentioned it. She has some old photographs of herself in the pilot's seat of these big old airplanes, her and some other women in uniform. She said they flew all kinds of warplanes across the country. She saw more military duty than many men in the service, but for years they never received any recognition from the government as veterans. I don't know if they'd even let her into a veteran's hospital. She'd never let me ask."

"Did she fly after the war?" the nurse asked.

"No, she became pregnant with me in 1945, and my father was killed over Germany. He was a fighter pilot. She never flew again. Rarely spoke of him."

"Did she remarry?"

"Yes, and he became my father. He died several years ago. I loved him, but I don't think they really ever got along too well together."

Suddenly, Barbara looked at the nurse. "I don't know why I told you that...I shouldn't have. Excuse me."

She stared at her mother, thin and still beneath the heavy covers. Only the occasional rise and fall of her chest indicating any life. "Please call me if anything..." She left the room in a hurry.

Eva unhooked the hem of her hospital gown from the rusty barb on the wire fence. Her bare feet pressed lightly into the dried weeds. Overhead, an airliner descended toward a runway three miles away, and Eva walked toward the old hangar on the deserted airstrip.

The scent of pine was heavy in the warm air, and she breathed in deeply. Passing a dusty pit full of beer cans and a shopping cart, she remembered a day in 1940 when a friend ground looped a Taylorcraft into it.

"Oh, they got into such an argument," she said aloud. "They eventually got married, you know," she said to no one. "George and Doris that is. He went off and flew bombers in the Pacific—B-24's.

She was the one who told me all about the WASP, talked me into joining. Last I heard they lived in New York, upstate somewhere. He's retired from TWA, I believe. She writes to me—a Christmas card every year..." Her voice trailed off as she stepped onto the deteriorated runway and stared at the wooden hangar.

Eva reached the chain link fence. Her legs grew heavy, her breath tight and short. She leaned against the fence.

"There was a grass strip that ran across the paved runway," she said. "We actually preferred the grass to the pavement. Every landing was a good one on grass. The flight examiners would make us land on the pavement, and, oh, how the tires would chirp and squeal. Showed us what sloppy landings we were really making. Did I mention I soloed here? In a Waco?"

She pushed away from the fence, stepped over a broken bottle and walked toward the hangar. Her pace quickened with each step.

"We had a Fairchild." She pointed toward a cluster of low trees. "There was another hangar there." The concrete base of the long-vanished hangar could be seen through the foliage.

"I took my instrument training in the Fairchild. Ed instructed in that, too." She looked away. A flight of robins lifted from the pine trees, circled over the runway, and in an undulating wave, returned to the woods. Eva continued toward the hangar.

She saw the rusted fuselage beneath the bullet riddled COCA COLA sign. The chipmunk sat unmoving, unaware of the snake beginning to coil along the welded tubing toward him.

"That's not the place to be," she tried to say, but the words stuck in her throat. The snake reached for the upper tube and, tongue probing the air, wound slowly toward the chipmunk.

Eva turned and ran. The bristled weeds clutched at her gown and legs. She reached the hangar completely out of breath and pressed her face against the wooden door. It gave. She stepped back and glanced over her shoulder at the fuselage where the chipmunk was about to be swallowed whole by the snake. She pressed on the door and followed it inside.

Late afternoon sunlight filtered through the many cracks in the ceiling, probing the still room with dusty yellow fingers. Eva's feet dragged through the grit and debris on the warped linoleum floor. A mouse scurried along a baseboard and disappeared through a crack.

A row of windows faced the abandoned runway. Most of the glass had been smashed out and plywood boards covered the holes. Eva's bare feet pressed into the glass shards without cutting.

"This was the pilot's lounge," she said. "That's where the model airplanes hung."

She swiped at the ceiling as though trying to set the imaginary models in motion.

"There was a couch across here, below the windows. Somebody was always trying to sleep there. And a table in the center of the room covered with magazines and charts and coffee cups.

"Whenever anyone soloed we would cut their shirt tail off and pin it to the walls around the room."

She twirled in a sweeping turn, her two arms taking in the whole room. Her face wore a bright distant smile.

"The instructor would print the date of the solo on the shirt tail and sign it. I complained when they cut mine, because it was my favorite blouse, but I really didn't mind, you know." She pointed. "It hung there. April 16th, 1940. And Ed's signature across the bottom.

"When he was cutting it out he made like he would accidentally snip through my bra strap. Well, of course, this made everyone laugh and applaud. My face turned the brightest red." She stared at the empty wall, where the paint was now peeling and water stains ran to the floor.

Something stirred outside—an engine barked. Eva turned.

"Wake up, Mrs. Gwyer," the nurse's voice cut through the deep fog in Eva's brain. "Wake up, I need to change your bedding." It was a different nurse, one she had never seen. The woman was tall and strong, yet gentle. She felt herself being lifted while fresh sheets were tucked under her weak and useless body.

"Why don't you let me alone?" she implored, her voice merely a croak.

The room was dark, except for the harsh direct light from above the bed. The nurse worked swiftly, effortlessly. Eva was jostled from side to side, allowing the nurse to make the bed one half at a time. The smell of starched white linen was strong in her nostrils.

"I was at the airport," she said. "I remember. I was there, just now." Eva gazed straight at the nurse who nodded and smiled while tucking in the corners, pulling the sheets drum tight.

"What airport was that, Mrs. Gwyer?"

Eva's face grew blank, confused by the question, as though the nurse had asked something completely absurd. "What airport was what?" Eva asked.

"You said you were at an airport," the nurse persisted. Somewhere beyond the doorway a phone rang, and a muffled voice answered it. Outside, the night sky flashed with diffused lightning. Eva turned toward the glass.

"It looks like rain tonight," the nurse said and pulled the sheets to Eva's chin. "Do you need anything?"

Eva stared into the friendly eyes, considering the question. Filled with sincerity, it fell woefully short of anything she could comprehend, and the answer formed in her mind but could not leave her mouth. "Do I need anything? Yes, I need everything. I need life, and health...and I want, no I long to look at the clouds."

The lightning flashed again. Eva turned back to the window and saw her reflection in the black glass, a hollow shadow, alone and tired. Suddenly, the night exploded in stark white, and she saw the trees lean against the initial blast of the storm. The window rattled from the boom of distant thunder drawing near.

"I want to fly," she said. "I want to fly again." She turned back to the nurse. "I used to fly. Ed taught me. Did you know him?"

"No."

She turned back to the dark window. Lightning tracked spider webs across the sky.

"Ed always wore an old leather jacket and smoked Chesterfields. He drove a motorcycle; it made such a racket. He'd run it right down the runway, racing the airplanes. Drove the airport manager—can't think of his name, ah, Bill something—drove him nuts." She turned to the nurse, who listened patiently, her face deeply creviced by the overhead light.

"Bill Cleverdon. That was his name, and Ed's motorcycle was an Indian. The first time he asked me out on a date I was terrified he'd show up on that bike, but somehow he borrowed Bill's Essex, and that was almost as bad. Seats were worn through, and you could look right between the rotten floorboards at the road whizzing past."

The nurse said nothing, only listened. She had done it many times before. It was all that was left to do.

Eva looked into the night. "Ed had thick wavy brown hair."

The sky rumbled, and fat raindrops, like tears, splattered against the glass, smearing her reflection.

"The Army shaved it all off when he went in, of course, but by the time he went overseas in '44 it had grown back—pretty much."

She was quiet. A telephone rang down the hallway again. Someone swept into the room, whispered to the nurse and left.

"Mrs. Gwyer, I have to go. You call if you need..." But Eva was staring at the rain and muttering to herself. The nurse left.

Water cascaded in sheets along the glass. Eva thought for a moment she was looking into a fast-moving river.

"Ed?" she called, raising herself on an elbow. "Do you remember the Waco? Do you remember how we flew it down the beach that summer?" She dropped heavily onto the pillow. Suddenly, the room was lighted with a bright white flash, and then plunged into shadows again. "We should do that again."

Eva tugged at her hospital gown caught on the barbed wire fence. It gave with a sharp rip, and she fell giggling to the weeds. Flat on her back, she gazed at the deep blue sky and watched chubby white clouds move slowly toward the horizon.

The air was heavy with pine; from somewhere in the distance the sweet chirp of a clarinet played Artie Shaw. She recognized the tune, or at least knew that she should remember it. She rose.

"What a beautiful day!" she exclaimed, and brushed stems and seeds from her gown. "Will you look at the way I'm dressed." She laughed aloud. One hand ran fingers through her suddenly long hair. The sound of a small airplane motor starting made her turn.

"Where are you?" she called. She started to run, her legs strong, eager to move. The sun pressed down, spreading vague warmth that also blinded her. She had trouble seeing where she was headed, or what was around her.

She found the runway, still crumbled and full of weeds, and at the limits of her hazy vision she could see the hangar past the chain link fence.

She glanced down at her gown, at her feet. They were melting out of focus. The clarinet played on. The airplane motor ticked in time with the music. She ran.

Overhead, an airliner descended, its jet engines whining. She turned, saw the aluminum skin glint in the sun, then, instantly, it vanished.

Eva no longer felt her body move; only the sensation of motion carried her along the runway toward the hangar and the source of the music.

The chain link fence was in sharp focus, blocking her path, and she reached out to grab it.

"Mrs. Gwyer," the voice called. She ran. "Mrs. Gwyer, do you hear me?"

"No!" Eva shouted, and the airport faded until the hospital room appeared in her vision. Two figures huddled together over her bed, and a third entered.

"How is she?" the third asked.

'Hello, Barbara,' Eva tried to say.

"Can she talk? Can she hear me?" her daughter asked, her questions sharp and to the point, the way she always spoke.

'Barbara, you're just going to have to loosen up a little, you're too damn serious.'

Someone poked her arm with a needle. The pain eluded her.

'Oh, don't waste your time, for crying out loud....'

The light faded, and she was at the airport.

"Mrs. Gwyer..." the voice persisted.

'Good bye,' Eva thought and reached for the chain link fence. It gave under her pressure, evaporating into air. She moved along the runway toward the hangar where the office door stood open.

"Close the door, Eva. You'll let all the flies out." The man's voice came from behind a counter near the source of the music. She pushed the door shut behind her, and a swarm of tiny airplanes suspended from the ceiling danced on the wind.

"Hello, Bill," she called. "What's that music?"

The man barely took form, beyond the little airplanes, but his voice came back, "Begin the Beguine?"

She nodded slowly and approached the window. Outside, the world was bright, and hazy figures appeared around a grass field dotted with airplanes.

"Is he out there?" she asked.

"See for yourself," Bill's voice answered.

Eva moved closer to the window, looking for the man in the leather jacket and wavy hair. Someone taxied a Cub past, and someone waved.

"Have I come to stay?" she asked Bill. He shrugged, his entire form still misty near the music. Eva turned back to the window, lifting herself onto the arm of a couch. She leaned against the cool glass, and from the corner of her vision saw the rusted fuselage alone in a patch of weeds.

She flinched. The chipmunk was there, atop the highest tube. The snake had curled its way unnoticed to a position directly behind it. Eva stared. She waited, as the snake, its tongue probing the air, sized up its prey. Like the chipmunk, she was unable to move.

Before she knew what happened, it struck.

She gasped. The music stopped. The chipmunk was gone. The snake eased down the tubing and disappeared, swallowing the image of the rusted fuselage with it. The music returned. The door behind her opened, and the little suspended airplanes bounced overhead. She stepped outside.

There, beyond the Cubs, past the Rearwin, the Taylorcraft and the Fairchild, stood the Waco. Its massive wings reached out for her, its silver propeller spun in a huge disk, reflecting the sun's glare.

And around the tail, stepped a man, dressed in a leather jacket and running his fingers through his wavy brown hair.

Chapter 6
ATC

"ATC Ghost Rider"

Twenty-five years as a controller, and, with 15 days until retirement, Jeffrey studied the radarscope, straining to keep awake. "Nighthauler 1236, three from MARVN, maintain 3000 until established on the localizer, cleared approach, tower 118.4...." The freight dog acknowledged and slid down the glideslope, leaving behind a radarscope sweeping an empty night sky. Jeffrey rubbed his eyes and muttered, "Still hate these graveyard shifts."

"Imagine how I feel."

Jeffrey shook his head and quickly checked for a stuck microphone button. The radio was fine, but he spotted a lone target cruising at 3000 feet across the radarscope and squawking an IFR code. Its data tag read: N645, a Bonanza. Jeffrey searched for flight progress data but found nothing.

"Don't know who I am, do you, Jeffery?"

"Ah...calling approach, say again?"

"C'mon, Jeffery, you must remember me."

The controller's skin flushed, realizing that he had an IFR target on his scope and had no idea who it was or where it was headed. He couldn't very well ask the pilot, "Excuse me, but who are you?"

"Name's Humphrey," the pilot offered, reading his thoughts. "Walter Humphrey." Before Jeffrey could answer, the pilot prompted, "Twenty-three years ago...remember?"

The sweat chilled, and Jeffrey could barely reply, "No...I don't remember."

The pilot laughed and didn't need to key the microphone to speak directly into Jeffrey's ear. "A night like this—overcast, no moon, sound familiar?"

Jeffrey answered, "No, you're talking to the wrong...you're on the wrong frequency. Stand-by."

"I've been standing by for twenty-three years, Jeffrey."

"Stop that! You don't know me."

"I do know that you fell asleep, leaving me on a radar vector to the localizer...."

"I was tired, and...and busy, but I wasn't asleep. You try working a mid-shift, alone, after a measly eight-hour break, see how sharp your mind is!"

"...and like a robot I just followed your vector right into that TV tower. Remember?"

Jeffrey shut his eyes tight. Yes, he remembered. Once again, he heard the open-mic crash sounds from years before. "No," he whispered. "I don't remember...besides, you should've known, should've questioned. Controllers aren't perfect."

"Supposed to be."

"And pilots are supposed to maintain situational awareness, not blindly trust the FAA to keep them out of trouble."

"Touché!"

"Wasn't my fault...not all my fault, anyhow."

"Never said it was, Jeffrey. You kept your job...."

"I was decertified, had to retrain and recertify. It was humiliating."

"I can only imagine...."

"Haven't had a deal since."

The frequency was silent until Jeffrey muttered; "I'm sorry," and he paused. "Is that good enough?" Receiving no answer, he looked up. The Bonanza's target faded, leaving only a ghost trail headed west across an empty radarscope.

The rest of the night held the usual bag of freighters, flying insomniacs and MEDEVAC helicopters. When his relief arrived, Jeffrey stowed his headset and stepped into the patchy dawn. Turning at the sound of an airplane taking off, he watched a Bonanza disappear into the broken clouds and started to smile. "Fourteen days to go."

© 2010

"Zzzzz...."

Alone in the approach control room at 2 A.M. The air hummed from radar scopes displaying no traffic and smelled like yesterday's coffee. I'd been there for three hours, had five to go and hadn't slept in almost 24. Anyone who's pulled guard duty knows that boredom is worse than fear. When controlling air traffic and threading a string of targets through a squall line your mind stays sharp, words shoot like M-16 rounds. But plop a controller in front of an empty scope for hours while the outside world sleeps, and the mind slips.

I'd just taken a handoff from Center, an IFR freighter on a VFR night, the pilot as tired as I was and probably just as bored. "Report the airport for a visual approach…" I said, and he mumbled, "Roger." Then, we sat, he in his airplane, and me staring at the radar sweep wiping the lone blip every seven seconds…every seven seconds…every zzzzz….

I jolted awake, sitting upright with eyes wide but not seeing. I glanced around trying to decide where I was. Was this real or another one of those dreams where I'm semi-naked and can't get the radar targets to respond to vectors?

Awake. Real. The wakening process didn't take more than a second, but as I looked at the scope I discovered it was empty. No freight dog, and the oath I then swore rhymes with "fit." I still had the IFR inbound's flight progress strip in front of me indicating it was active—but no airplane. I keyed my mic and cautiously asked, "Freightair twelve-ten, say altitude." No answer. I asked again with the same result. As I keyed the mic to ask a third time in some desperate hope that by calling he'd reappear, the controller in the tower called down over the hot line: "You looking for Freightair?" I admitted I was, and she laughed saying, "He landed ten minutes ago!"

No harm, no foul, and no on reported my unplanned nap. But it scared the hell outa me. I was 37 years old and liked being a controller but hated mid-shifts.

Mids came at the end of a weirdly compressed workweek that began on Monday afternoon at 3. With each succeeding day the shift started earlier until by Thursday I'd report to the tower at 6 A.M., work until 2 P.M., go home—never get any sleep—and return that night at 11 for the mid. By dawn Friday when the freight dogs swarmed in, and the airlines pushed back, a graveyard controller would be punchy while working the morning rush. The night I lost the freighter I was lucky to be working a "two-man" mid—one in the tower, one in the TRACON. Grace, the other "man" saved me. But too often we'd work alone combining approach, tower, ground and clearance delivery. Easy when the traffic keeps flowing. The stress keeps you awake. But stare at an empty sky for hours on end and say goodnight, Gracie.

© 2011

"Extend Yer Downwind"

Lee couldn't sit when he worked traffic—so many airplanes, too much fun. "Isn't being a controller stressful?" non-controllers would ask at parties where no one knew anything about aviation. "Yeah, but it's good stress," Lee always answered. Meaning, "You couldn't possibly understand how cool it is to stand in a control tower, manipulating a sky full of airplanes. "The real stress," he'd add, "comes from working for the FAA."

It was late 1981, months after the PATCO strike, and a million years since 11,000 fired controllers had faded into old news. Lee had transferred from flight service and loved the change. No more parroting, "VFR not recommended," to pilots, who, he suspected, didn't know a prog chart from a convective SIGMET. Working air traffic at Reid-Hillview Airport was like swimming inside a blender with endless Cessnas, Cubs, Champs, T-crafts and the occasional Ford Tri-Motor vying for the parallel runways.

Lee talked non-stop: "Cessna 76G, number four, follow the Apache...Taylorcraft 835, if you hear me, rock your wings...I see that, runway 30L, cleared touch-and-go...Cherokee 52N, extend yer downwind, I'll call base..." And it all worked provided he maintained the jazz rhythm that energizes ATC. Miss a beat, and you vamp like mad to regain it. Miss too many, and you're down the tubes gasping for air.

"Breaktime." Lee swiveled to see Kathleen already writing call signs on a pad of paper. Together they scanned the pattern as Lee conveyed the traffic flick: "Robin's in the T-crate, cleared touch 'n go on the left. The Apache is cleared to land on the right with Cessna 76G behind it..." Until Kathleen said, "Got it," and Lee replied, "You got it."

Transfer complete, Lee lingered to review the checklist, ensuring he hadn't forgotten anything. But within minutes the picture had changed. Kathleen was in the groove, clearing, sequencing and barely pausing to sip her coffee. Lee tossed his headset onto the counter before heading downstairs. He glanced over his shoulder thinking, "Feel like I forgot something..." Shrugged and left.

He didn't notice that the first step down took him 30 years ahead, where, now, he was Reid-Hillview's tower chief about to retire. He'd been a good player. He'd climbed the career ladder through other

ATC facilities and returned to finish where he'd begun. It worked perfectly, until he suddenly sat upright in bed, damp with sweat. "Oh no…"

"What is it?" Kathleen asked, barely awake.

"Forgot something," Lee answered. "Go back to sleep." And he bolted from bed.

Thirty minutes later, Lee unlocked the dark control tower and climbed four stories to the cab. The airport's beacon pulsed through the glass, while the ATIS looped, "…control tower is closed until…" Slowly Lee scanned the empty traffic pattern, picked up a microphone and, gazing at the stars, called, "Cherokee 52N, turn base, cleared to land." And from the far side of the moon a voice responded, "Request touch and go." To which Lee replied, "Unable. This nightmare ends now!" Only then, could he sit.

© 2011

Chapter 7
California Flyin'

"The Commute"

The drive from Watsonville, California on the ocean side of the Santa Cruz Mountains to Reid Hillview Airport in San Jose, took an hour. If the coastal fog wasn't in, and I flew the Aeronca Champ, it'd take slightly longer. Flying to work wasn't meant to save time. It was all about making the commute the high point of the day, and cresting the ridge at Mt. Madonna on a summer morning offered the perfect beginning.

It's been over twenty years since I worked in the Reid Hillview control tower, but that tiny airfield imprinted magic inside my head. At dawn I'd ride my Triumph motorcycle to Watsonville Muni, preflight the Champ and hand-prop it to start. By the time I taxied and departed, at least twenty minutes of the commute was gone. Climbing across the orchards toward the hills, I'd always marvel at what was possibly the most beautiful spot on Earth. Popping over the redwood trees I'd begin a slow descent across wide pastures to intercept the freeway. It led to a patch of aviation splendor hemmed in by houses and a shopping center relentlessly trying to strangle this dream to death.

By the time I tied down and walked to the tower, over an hour would've elapsed. The first leg of my commute was complete, and I'd spend the next eight hours being paid to watch others fly. It was nothing short of stealing. From my skybox seat I'd watch Amelia Reid's fleet of Taylorcrafts flit about like dragonflies. Armed with barely audible radios, her students became experts at light gun signals. There was little IFR traffic, and it wasn't uncommon to record a hundred VFR operations per hour. "Cleared to land...cleared touch-and-go...number three follow the Ford Tri-motor, caution wake turbulence." Technically, we were air traffic controllers but felt more like air ringmasters and occasionally referees breaking the ties. "That ain't gonna work, so, Stinson, go around, make left closed traffic and quit whining."

It was more than an airport. It was a place where countless dreams came true every day when ordinary lives found lift. And, at the end of my shift I'd sign off the air with: "Attention all aircraft, the tower's closed." If Robin Reid was in the pattern with a radio that actually worked there might be friendly, " 'bout time; need help starting the Champ?"

I rarely needed help, but at Reid Hillview Airport, there was always someone there to offer it. Despite being an FAAer, I felt like an honored guest in the Reid's aviation backyard. And as the sun reached for the Monterey Bay, I'd climb back across the mountains hoping that the fog hadn't arrived for the night. Often it did, and I'd run through Chittendon Pass and follow the river into town. After touchdown, when I taxied for the hangar, I'd grin without a trace of guilt, knowing I had the greatest commute above the world. Best of all—I always looked forward to doing it again the next day.

© 2006

"Pilo 's Lounge"

The letter T disappeared from the Watsonville airport pilot's lounge door in 1978. The resulting Pilo 's Lounge read like a Latin nightclub run by a sultry temptress named Pilo. So, that's what Vern, the cigar-smoking airport manager and former Navy pilot, named the cat that walked into the terminal like Lauren Bacall in a white fur warp. Being a cat, the fur was her own, but being Bacall, she knew how to use it, and Vern fell for Pilo the way Bogie fell for Bacall.

Her green eyes flashed the indifference women reserve for men who try too hard to impress. As pilots sat around the lounge talking with their hands about hammerheads, spins, and crosswind landings, she'd yawn and watch the runway for Vern. She was too classy for a pimply ramp rat like me who cleaned toilets, fueled airplanes and couldn't believe I was getting paid to hang around an airport.

Then on a wet January afternoon a Mitsubishi MU2 turboprop taxied onto the ramp. I waved it between two parking spaces, because I was really crappy at directing traffic. It swung its tail the way a shark might when angling for dinner as the propellers screamed with the shrill of a blender wanting to puree me.

Barely had the props spun down when the pilot opened the door so his passengers wouldn't have to wait a half-second more than their important lives could bear. I said, "Hello," as they passed, but they looked through me for the better things that they knew they deserved. He was in that middle range of years when white shoes seemed appropriate while she looked artificially younger, wore a tight skirt and smelled of lavender, which reminded me to replace the urinal cakes in the men's room.

Later, when I returned to the office after fueling the MU2, I saw Pilo curled like a white croissant into the lavender woman's lap. She tapped her husband's arm with a long, painted finger nail and quickly indicated with a curled lip slathered in ruby grease that he should talk to me, which he did. "Hey, kid, give ya twenty bucks for that cat. The wife wants it."

"Not mine to sell," I explained, although I could've used the double sawbuck he'd peeled from a wad of bills the size of a hay bale. "She's the airport cat, belongs to…well, to the airport." And the husband shrugged and walked away with an expression that said he'd tried, and that "the wife" shouldn't have to suffer.

It rained all afternoon, and the visibility dropped so low over the Monterey Bay after sunset that no one saw the Mitsubishi depart. The letter T was never replaced on the pilot's lounge door and likewise, Pilo, the airport cat, was never seen again. We knew who took her, and, now, all these years later, when I catch a whiff of jet fuel and lavender, I look around for that MU2, because Vern still wants his cat back.

© 2004

"Confessions of a Ramp Rat"

In 1977 I made my mark on aviation as an airport attendant—a janitor with a fuel truck—at the Watsonville, California Municipal Airport. It was the week before the Memorial Day fly-in, and the ramp was abuzz with anticipation, like New Orleans preparing for a hurricane only with less music and more beer. A pilot asked me to top off his Bonanza so he could get out of town before the event. I ran to the fuel truck, ground the gears and lurched toward the T-hangars. As I pulled in front of the Bonanza's hangar, I shifted into neutral and was about to engage the fuel pump when I paused to consider whether the Bonanza took 100 or 80 octane. The truck dispensed 80 from one side and 100 on the other, so I hopped from the cab and slipped inside the hangar where a quick look at the caps confirmed—100 octane.

Normally, I'd, then, reel out the hose, but when I turned I was surprised to see the 2000-gallon, bright yellow truck was gone. Something that size is hard to misplace, but it wasn't there. And that's when I remembered that under normal conditions I would've set the emergency brake before getting out of the cab. Being distracted, though, I hadn't. Mystery solved.

The truck was rolling—unattended—down the ramp toward the drainage ditch. Panicked, I ran after it shouting, "Stop!" Upon reflection, that made little sense but, then chasing a giant liquid bomb made no sense either. So, I stopped to watch the fuel truck bounce through the drainage ditch like a yellow whale trying to hump the fence on the other side. It lunged forward, paused, and rocked back, accelerated by the sloshing fuel and somewhat slowed by its underside scraping the concrete. When it finally came to rest I climbed aboard and calmly backed away from the bent fence. That wasn't my mark.

Safety-conscious after my near-napalm moment, I slowly drove around the southeast end of the hangar to re-attempt fueling the Bonanza. As I tuned the wheel, while looking to my left to avoid squashing an EAAer frantically pushing his Thorpe T-18 out of my way, I heard a screeching noise like giant fingernails on a chalkboard. Or like a fuel track dragging its flanks along a hangar.

We tend to remember those aviation greats who leave their marks by setting altitude records or rescuing Berliners from Commie Russians. But how often have you stopped to salute the ramp rat who just fueled your Centurion and then, say, backed over his own stepladder? I'll save my stepladder confession for another time, but if you attend the Watsonville Fly-in (now Labor Day weekend), find the row of T-hangars northeast of the terminal. They usually try to hide it, but sneak behind the row of port-a-crappers and you'll see the mark I left on aviation and the hangar corner. It's been a heavy burden, but after three decades I couldn't keep my secret any longer. Closure, at last.

© 2007

"Irrational Behavior"

She's older now than the airplane had been on the day they'd met. Back then, as she read the index card on the Calaveras County Airport bulletin board, Victoria thought, "Why not?" And three days later, after a pleading trip to the credit union, she owned the Aeronca

Chief with its yellow rudder and a faded red band around a pale blue waist reminding her of a tired matador. Leaning from a soft landing-gear strut, he looked to be sweeping his cape—gallant, untouched by age, and ready to win a lady's heart.

Back home inside a metal hangar, she painted a bull on the vertical fin and over its snorting face the word, Ole'. Except what she envisioned as a charging bull others saw more as a Norwegian moose.

"Who's Olie?" a neighbor asked, and, then, before she could explain, he added while turning to leave, "Ya know, you probably coulda got yourself a nice Cherokee instead."

The "coulda" hung in the air. It was so easy to fling a "coulda" without knowing where it might land. Victoria looked at her matador and felt doubt seep into her heart. She coulda bought something practical with IFR radios, lights and seats in the back that few pilots ever filled. She coulda done that and woulda been safe from criticism for having ventured beyond the norm.

The wind rattled the hangar's tin, and a Stellar Jay flew under the open door, looked around, and, then, as though seeing her winged bull-moose, it accused her of, "Coulda, coulda..." and escaped to warn other birds of Victoria's mistake.

But pushing the Chief through the open door, Victoria felt the airplane pulse as the wings grabbed at the hot wind. Sunlight washed over the fuselage that she'd spent the morning waxing and brushed her cheek with a dusty softness she was beginning to understand.

She tied the tail and clicked the mag switch on. Alone on the empty ramp, she swung the wooden propeller, and the engine cracked to life with the sound of flamenco heels on a marble floor. Moving around the wing, she ran her hand lightly along the lowered tip where the weak gear strut couldn't hold it any higher; then she slipped into the left seat and fastened the straps after closing the door.

The wind nudged them off centerline on takeoff, and she countered with aileron. Climbing away from the hot earth they were tossed as she walked the rudders searching for the dance's rhythm. The engine sang, the propeller grabbed for air, and they banked into a steep turn over the valley and toward the nearby hills where she said aloud to the hawks circling in the thermals: "I coulda...but why would I ever wanna fly anything else?"

They were both younger then, she older than he. But now, their ages have joined. Victoria loves her matador, and she doesn't care what others think, because some people just can't grasp the truth about flight — the dance of irrational love.

© 2004

"Open Cockpit Mind"

It's motorcycling in the sky. To a car driver traveling along a coastal highway the scenery offers a pretty backdrop to an air-conditioned journey between two points, but to the motorcyclist who leans through the curves and feels the air, cool through the misty valleys and warm over the ridges, the destination is irrelevant. The rider arrives invigorated while the driver merely gets there. Likewise, open-cockpit flight has little to do with transportation and is more about getting somewhere unreachable.

Flying with nothing between you and the sky is vastly different than flight inside a cabin where your scan is too easily focused on a GPS map instead of the world itself. Inside a biplane without a lid to contain your mind, hurricanes rip past the windscreen where its thin layer of clear plastic creates a cocoon of leeward tranquility. With your senses peeking above the cockpit's rim you're as alone as anyone can be and, yet, feel as though the entire universe of wind, cloud, and that hawk circling off your wings belongs to you. Tempted, you'll reach a gloved hand toward the vision only to have the wind remind you of the soft violence that creates and protects this image.

There is no straight-and-level in open cockpit flying. When seated behind two sets of fabric wings reflecting sunlight, you can't help but bank to capture a stray cloud shaped like tomorrow's memory. You'll pitch up to the edge of a stall, hover, and make the earth fall off your mind into a spin. Close the throttle, pull up, and hear the flying wires chant your song that varies with every twitch of the joystick. You're the aerial choirmaster, composer, and audience with the sky for a stage.

There is no purpose to open-cockpit flying; common sense long ago deemed it inefficient. Excessive drag and numbing cold made it impractical. The wind's fury coaxed pilots indoor where they could better interpret dials, sort through charts, and follow air traffic control's lead. The pilot whose head pokes into the sky finds it tough to follow anyone's lead, because when you immerse yourself in the above, you'll discover an atmosphere that ignores linear thought and devours all dimensions at once.

Open-cockpit flying isn't the end of the journey or the only route along it. You won't lift off with your goggled eyes flashing and instantly discover all the answers you've sought through flight. You may not even see the questions. Instead, when you taxi down a grass runway, S-turning from left to right while leaning over the cockpit's rim to see what's ahead, you'll hear the rumble of past aviators who once flew exactly as you now do. When you open the throttle and lift off the ground as dust and bits of cornstalk slip inside the cockpit to twirl around like angry sprites, you'll know why flight without doors is not for practical minds but, instead, is open to those who ride alone on the edge of all the other possibilities.

© 2005

"Civil Twilight"

The 26th was circled in merlot red on Hal's calendar taped to his hangar wall. It was from an avionics dealer and showed a photo of a 1938 Spartan Executive for February. The silver monoplane banked over a late afternoon vineyard near Santa Ynez, California indicating that life is good when the wine is properly served. Or at least that was Hal's philosophy, and each afternoon as the sun dissolved into the Monterey Bay, 200 miles northwest of Santa Ynez, Hal would declare the flying day over and pour a glass of red wine or white if the day had been unusually warm. He'd pour two or more if visitors showed.

February 26 is St. Timothy's day. "He's the patron saint of sitting around with purpose," Hal would tell anyone drawn to the hangar by his 1946 Taylorcraft. Hal didn't speak much, but he liked to quote St. Paul's advice to Timothy: "Drink no longer water, but use a little wine for thy stomach's sake and thine other infirmities." Then as he slowly packed his pipe, he'd add, "Chapter five, verse twenty-three," and you suspected it was the only Biblical passage he knew or had ever read. Then again, when a man finds solace why continue the search? Whatever the time of year at Watsonville Municipal Airport, other infirmities such as bad landings, the threatening development of the surrounding lettuce fields or fog that brings a VFR day to a fuzzy halt, were easily handled with the aged grape in a lawn chair beneath a wing.

Hal believed in the simple excellence of aviation—the lovingly constructed homebuilt or a fabric job so beautiful you could barely see the tapes through a candy-coated finish. When he flew, which was almost daily, he did so with unrushed passion. The throttle advanced with the steady squeeze of a marksman's finger on a trigger as though coaxing each horse beneath the cowling to run its best. Cruising across the Santa Cruz Mountain ridges the T-craft was a condor, endangered by a world that insisted on progress or at least purpose. His landings were clouds returning to earth—unhurried yet touching exactly where nature intended.

Flight to Hal was the purpose; any transportation from points A to B was merely a lucky byproduct. The Spartan in the calendar photo, although a cabin-class brute born to carry important humans to equally important destinations, never actually went anywhere in his world but, instead, remained forever frozen in that glorious bank above the vines, reminding the viewer that all journeys returned to this hangar where civility of mind was open to anyone willing to escape on wings and return to a respectable cabernet served in the company of like minds that never truly belong on the planet for longer than it takes to refuel.

So mark your calendars—not just for February 26, but also for every twenty-sixth day of your life and, then, pour the wine, sit with your airplane, and drink to the civil twilight.

© 2005

"On Little Cat Wings"

The world's rough edges are rounded smooth in fog. Or so Jake felt, walking down a row of flight school airplanes, damp in the enveloping gray. The students had left hours ago. Jake glanced over his shoulder as one of his flight instructors started her car, waved and pulled from the lot. Yellow headlights smeared through the mist, pulling her into monochrome oblivion. Jake smiled, because after a full day of flying he cherished this time alone on the silent airport.

But he was never completely alone. Sandburg, the airport cat, attacked from beneath a Comanche's wing and joined him on his walk. Together they checked tie-down ropes, several knots loose from students in too big a hurry to pull them tight. The cat rubbed against a tail wheel as Jake opened a Cessna 140's door and snapped off the master switch. "Mixture, master, mags," he reminded the cat, who'd heard it before. "That's what my old boss, Vern, once told me..." and his voice trailed away, remembering the day he'd ferried the airplane to the flight school, years before. The cat knew the story well, including how Jake had skirted a snowstorm over southwestern Kansas and across the Oklahoma Panhandle. How he'd become lost when drawn to the lights of Marfa, Texas and landed in Mexico where he had to pay a federale for directions back across the border. When he'd arrived home ten days later with the new, and now filthy, Cessna, Vern didn't ask what had taken so long. Instead, he simply reached inside the cockpit, snapped off the master switch Jake had forgotten and chanted, "Mixture, master, mags."

Jake and Sandburg continued their airport inspection, checking hangar doors and the front gate. When they circled back to the edge of the tie-down ramp, the cat sat beside Jake on the fuel truck's running board. Like twin Buddas they stared into the mist at another day turned into night. Except for the pink glow of nearby harbor and city slashed by the airport beacon's sweep, there was no other light. And no sound except a distant surf.

Jake loved to teach and loved being a part of the airfield since he'd left the Army. He cherished the Thanksgiving visits from students who'd become pilots for Braniff, Pan-Am and TWA. Their futures were bright, while his remained comfortably socked in, flying the same airplanes while reciting the same lessons, such as: "Mixture, master, mags." Periodically, someone would ask: "Don't you ever want to fly jets?" And few believed how content he was with what he had.

Another year was fading, and beyond that fog loomed 1960, promising a kerosene-burning era when life would launch into stratospheric possibilities. But Jake, whose soul belonged in piston taildraggers, wasn't quite ready, so he turned to the cat and asked, "Time to move on?" Sandburg ignored this human misinterpretation of time and unwarranted need to reestablish the world's rough edges. "Sorry," Jake apologized and continued to sit, absorbed in perfect airport silence.

© 2008

Chapter 8
Mid-American Skies

"Between Storms"

With the sound of oatmeal squeezed through a banana peel, mud sucked the sneaker off my foot leaving me to dance one-legged until I retrieved the shoe and fell sideways against the hangar with a kettledrum Bong that no doubt impressed Courtenay, a client already apprehensive about flying with thunderstorms roaming the area.

"Oh, that line's well to the east of us," I reassured her while flushing my tennis shoe beneath the downspout. "Thunderstorms move in from the west," and I pointed the soggy shoe toward advancing blue sky trimmed with marshmallow clouds. "Gives us plenty of time to practice a few crosswind landings." And hopping on one foot, I pulled on my sneaker and smiled. Besides a smooth personal demeanor, flight instructing in thunderstorm alley demands a dual appreciation of rapidly changing skies and the serenity found in chaos. So, each on a strut, we pushed her 1941 Interstate Cadet—imagine a tall Cub with superb manners—onto the wet grass and tied the tail to a rusty eyehook with a frayed rope normally used to tether the airport dog when not restraining hand-propped taildraggers. The rain had quit, but the retreating squall line rumbled in the distance like a biker gang moving on to the next tavern, its backside a wall of lightning-etched showers tossing mobile homes across green pastures like dice on a blackjack table. I ducked beneath a wing, smacked my forehead on the doorframe and fell into the rear seat.

"Brakes on. Contact!" she called, and I repeated before she spun the wood prop by hand to spark the Continental engine awake. After untying the tail she climbed into the front seat and shoved the side window closed.

"No, leave it open," I said. "So you can smell the sky; it's beautiful after a rain." She did, and we back-taxied down the runway splashing rooster tails behind the tires in parallel ruts through the grass. Courtenay swung the tail with gentle rudder and a breath of power in her left hand to align with the runway. She paused and then inched the throttle full. Even heavy, the Interstate used almost no runway to leave the earth. Lift pulled our wheels from the turf, and with aileron against the crosswind and opposite rudder to track straight, Courtenay lowered the nose in ground effect for airspeed, gently pulled back on the stick and coordinated the controls so the Interstate weather-vaned into a perfect crab angle to climb. By then she'd relaxed and felt the airplane explain what it needed in a sky scrubbed clean by the passing storms.

Every sky has a unique personality, and when a thunderstorm strides across the prairie, we tiny winged creatures avoid its footfalls. It'll kill without remorse, but as Courtenay discovered, there's intense beauty in a storm's wake — clear air laced with mountains of sun-streaked white against blue so intense it'll suck any dullness from your head leaving behind a reminder of what makes some of us get our feet wet.

© 2006

"Winter of Discontent Dies"

Richard's boots sucked muddy water with each step across the sod ramp. His damp feet grew colder, but he kept moving as though stalking something wounded. He slipped beneath a Cessna Cardinal, parked since Thanksgiving when a couple from Alamogordo had arrived "for the weekend." On short final they'd hit a wild turkey—the irony was priceless—and returned home on the airlines. Richard was supposed to have repaired the damage, but the weather dictated otherwise, so there it sat, prisoner of a vicious winter that was dying, as all tyrants must. Richard secretly wished winter an agonizing death, because he hated the cold. Bing and Danny could sing about snow all they wanted, but this grassroots FBO on the Prairie had no love of white runways.

The wind, though, had shifted on April First. Warm and dry it blew in from the southwest, perhaps with a plea from the Alamogordo pilots to "Let our Cardinal go." Perhaps not. Winter plays tricks on a mechanic's mind. Richard untied the airplane, dropped the frayed ropes into the mud and stared at the cantilever wing and low-rider windshield. He quietly admired Cessna's attention to grace and form in this uniquely American design. Even now, with her tires nearly flat and skin encrusted in winter grime, her curves showed through. Like her older cousin, the 195, the Cessna 177 was a sexy airplane. Few airplanes could say that, and fewer mechanics ever said it aloud. Richard quickly glanced over his shoulder; worried someone might've heard his thoughts. But he was alone with the dry wind and grinned as he went for the tractor to pull the Cardinal into the shop.

He left the hangar door open and parked the airplane over the floor drain. With garden hose in hand he climbed atop a stepladder, opened the nozzle and soaked the airframe. Winter grime dissolved and swirled away, taking the last bits of Thanksgiving turkey from the cowling. And when Richard inspected the damage it wasn't as bad as he'd originally thought. Nothing is when spring arrives.

Repairs took two days, during which the wind completely vanquished winter. On the third day, Richard tugged the airplane outside and was about to climb in when he stopped to wipe his shoes. The wind tried to snatch the wide Cardinal door from his hand, but he held fast and slipped inside to run up the engine. In 29 years on the field he'd never learned to fly. He knew so much about it, but diabetes—an injustice he'd never understand—kept him wrenching, not flying.

The Alamogordo couple arrived looking happy in that blank way people have who've never wrestled winter to the mat. Richard happily took their money, and they happily took off. Inside the shop, again, a radio above the workbench finished playing Stravinsky's The Rite of Spring, when the announcer casually mentioned a "chance of snow." And just as casually Richard's ball peen hammer amended its wintry forecast into shattered bits of discontent.

© 2008

"Sundogs and Biplanes"

It's hard to imagine life without wings, I thought while walking through ankle-deep snow toward the hangar. Without them, I'd be in bed instead of watching the sun rise over the wind tee catching a pair of sundogs dancing shamelessly against a pink-blue backdrop. These rainbow apparitions float like silly promises in the sky when the air is too cold to hold a moist thought. Those who sleep without wings on winter mornings can't see this and shuffle eyes-down through life with warm feet and dull hearts.

Pilots can't walk four steps without looking up to find clouds that need busting or to identify a distant engine—is it a Lycoming or Continental? A Jacobs radial or long-nosed Merlin will empty a hangar as pilots tilt faces upward with each mind a part of a collective aviation fantasy.

But I was alone as the hangar door gave with a jagged groan of cracking ice. My breath steamed in a shaft of pure morning light that displayed the Marquart biplane inside like a graying stage actor awaiting its cue to go on. Its nose was wrapped in a red blanket to capture heat from an electric furnace that groaned between the gear legs. I'd plugged the heater in before dawn, and two hours later, with the sky as cold as creation I peeled back the blanket, snapped open the cowling and found spring.

The winter preflight ritual is slow. In summer, the airplane's molecules buzz and jump, impatient to turn steel and fabric into flight. But as temperatures drop to where even ice skaters say, "Damn it's cold," time itself crawls. I slid the oil dipstick from its scabbard and watched the 40-weight honey slide back into the engine like warm blood and knew that flight was possible. Not only possible, I anticipated it would be glorious beyond imagination in air so dense that even wheezy old cylinders would produce more power while the biplane's four swept-back wings lunged for the sky with the grasp of an Olympic butterfly swimmer. While there's a price to pay for winter flight, the rewards abound.

Preheat quickly died once I pushed the biplane from the hangar and removed the thermal blanket. I could almost hear the engine metals contract as I swung my booted foot across the cockpit's rim and dropped onto the rock-cold seat cushion. My gloved hands snapped the master and fuel pump switches on and worked the primer to inject icy adrenaline into the intake manifold. I pumped a full stroke on the throttle stiff with cold, and shouted, "Clear prop," to an empty ramp. Then, with visions of my wings tilting with sundogs, I pressed the starter button to unleash the unholy sound of a solenoid clicking—Kek, kek, kek, kek....

An open cockpit is a cold place to contemplate life without wings, but with sundogs dancing into oblivion overhead, I knew that because of a dead battery, contemplation was all I'd get on this winter morning.

© 2004

"Ski-Fly"

Snow curled beneath the hangar door, crossed the gravel floor past spent oilcans and dusted the Aeronca Chief's wood skis, like clown's feet, where tires normally attached.

"Federals," Lars, the ski-fly instructor, noted with a nod of his head deep inside his parka. I didn't know diddly about airplane-skiing but nodded back at the name Federal. It's like hearing "Whipline" when talking floats. I tend to nod knowingly when clueless; something I'd mastered working for the FAA.

Lars removed a mitten and shoved his bare hand beneath the thermal blanket around the engine. "She's ready," he announced the way a large animal vet might when examining a heifer. "Get the door, will ya?" It wasn't a question. If we were to ski-fly the fresh powder that had fallen overnight we'd have to free the hangar door, which was stuck to the ground. I pressed myself against it as Lars called, "Puuush…" and chipped with a pickax at the frozen dirt beneath. The hangar groaned when I slammed my padded shoulder against the door, and it gave with a bony crack that I feared was my spine until the door swung wide and pink sunshine washed the little airplane center stage.

Panting, I wondered how we'd move an airplane without wheels from inside to out, when Lars indicated parallel strips of packed snow leading to each ski over which the airplane could slide. I nodded, realizing that there's nothing easy about winter flying: Preheat takes hours if done correctly, instruments respond sluggishly, and hand-propping a Continental engine while standing flat-footed on ice can lead to pilots getting nicknamed, "Stumpy."

After a few shots on the engine primer, like injecting Jack Daniels down a cadaver's throat, Lars snapped the propeller blade, and the engine fired to life. "Carb heat on and give 'er another squirt of gas if she dies," he yelled over the arctic prop blast. His words vanished in the wind, and the airplane shifted when he climbed in beside me. We squeezed together like two Michelin tire men stealing a Finnish Volkswagen.

"Oil pressure didn't come up right away," I worried aloud. He shrugged, so I added, "And the temp's barely off the peg."

"It will be by June," he said, and, again, I nodded.

When finally we took the runway after a Super Cub had departed, I stared down the vast expanse of brilliant white and opened the throttle. The Chief's plywood feet slapped frozen divots hidden beneath the snow. Distracted, I lost directional control and, as with float flying, discovered that brakes are nonexistent on skis. We swerved between runway lights and over the corn stubble causing Lars to remark, "The goal in ski flying is to get the skis off da ground, yah?" Again, it wasn't a question, so I pulled back on the yoke, cleared the fence, and as I looked down at crystals misting off a Federal ski above a frozen planet, I nodded and thought: "Some things shouldn't be understood but relished instead."

©2005

"Why Me?"

The first cutting of hay lay in flat windrows beside the asphalt runway. Kate's biplane taxied from the hangar and paused at the hold-short lines where she pushed her goggles above her eyes and leaned her face into the idling slipstream. She inhaled the sweet blast of spring. It tasted of new growth and burnt avgas, and she swirled it around in her head before exhaling. After a miserably long winter flying iced-up freight charters in a tired Aztec she deserved a sunny morning to herself. And then, because she wasn't about to let anyone tell her how to behave on her own airport, she taxied across the pavement and onto the grass.

Daryl was at the far end of the field, he and the tractor framed between struts and flying wires. He'd turned around to begin another pass through the hay when he spotted Kate. He spun the old International in a wide circle as though to say, "Cleared for takeoff." So Kate pulled down her goggles, opened the throttle and squeezed right rudder while lifting the tail.

Daryl watched the biplane track straight between the windrows. Wingtip vortices fluffed the hay in its wake. He waved his cap at the airplane's underbelly, and Kate rocked her wings before banking toward the hills. Daryl knew he'd have to re-rake the hay she'd disturbed, but it didn't matter. With her, it never did.

Kate glanced back, thinking that four decades was a long time to fly from the same airfield. After thousands of takeoffs, guiding countless students around the traffic pattern she wondered why it could still seem new. "How," she thought, "can I feel like I did when I first soloed here all those years ago?" She had no answer and considered if one even existed. Then, looking between the flying wires toward the soft green ridgeline she knew she could never stop asking.

Below, Daryl turned back for another pass. In a few days he'd bale the hay, and Kate would use the field as a grass runway until it grew too tall again. She'd begin new students in the rental Cessnas, reciting the same, "This is an airplane," introductory lesson. And each evening she and Daryl would refuel their tiny fleet, discuss which ones he could repair and which were worn out and ready for the sale barn. They'd talk money over supper, mostly how to stretch fewer dollars against steeper expenses. And they'd sleep together in the yellow house beside the hangar at the end of the field.

They'd repeat the cycle that led to Kate now pulling the biplane's nose high above the horizon. And as she arced through a lazy wingover, momentarily suspended in time, she studied their little airport with its faded hangars and skinny black runway. Beside it a bright red tractor etched neat rows of hay. Looking down upon absolute perfection Kate knew she'd never understand why she was so blessed. And, falling back to earth, she never felt more grateful.

© 2010

"It's a Flat Earth After All"

We meet at the airport at no specified time because we wouldn't want anyone to feel rushed or late. The meeting is called to order when the first airplane takes off from the grass. The minutes aren't read because no one writes them down. We don't have a treasury, because most of us are broke from the last overhaul, a recent recover, or insurance premium spike. Yet, despite this apparent lack of organization, we seem to accomplish our one goal-to verify that the world is flat.

We're the Greater Midwest Tailwheeling Flat Earth Society, and we meet whenever the sky is clear with the horizon a straightedge from wing tip to wing tip. Meetings are open to anyone willing to climb aboard an old airplane that rarely goes above 1500 feet; anything higher than that and you can't really tell that the Earth is flat.

And it is. Sure, NASA has pictures that offer a convincing argument that we live on a blue rock in a limitless cosmos, but that's just scientific proof, which has little to do with the nature of flight. Is it science that drew you to your first flying lesson? Does science make you fall in love with beauty so intense it can't be kept on the ground?

Try this experiment: Take off one evening when the sun rests like a flaming volleyball on the rim of the planet. Throttle back, bring the nose up, and just before the airspeed tickles the stall, kick in left rudder. Watch the horizon rock its wings at you as you break left and it breaks right. It can do that because it's flat.

It's all a hoax, really, this notion of a round planet. I know because I've spread a sectional chart on the grass beneath the wing of my airplane as dawn seeped above the horizon. Without moving from my sleeping bag, I've shot a course across the flat sectional with a stubby pencil, then measured the distance with my outstretched fingers: A full octave from pinky tip to thumb is 60 miles, a finger width is five miles, and two fingers are ten miles. It's my Flat Earth Positioning System (FEPS), that requires no satellites—which I don't believe in—no batteries, and best of all, with Flat Earth navigation you never return to the same spot twice. Each flight is a journey with no destination known. Others may think you've returned to your hangar at the end of the day, but they're blinded by scientific data.

To prove that the Earth is flat, take a nonbeliever aloft on an autumn morning. As the dew streams back in the prop blast, and the wheels leave the ground, watch that horizon stretch like a straight smile that welcomes you to the sky.

Unfortunately, many will refuse to consider the possibility of limitless horizon. And that's why we hold regular meetings of the Greater Midwest Tailwheeling Flat Earth Society. You're always welcome to attend. But don't wait too long, because we might start the meeting without you.

© 2002

"Biplanes To Blakesburg"

Banking left, I glanced over the biplane's open-cockpit rim at two grass runways that carved an X in the wooded hills and late summer corn. The east/west strip was closed for arrivals and, instead, covered with parked airplanes. Old airplanes. Hundreds of 'em.

From 700 feet up, I saw a Stinson Tri-Motor beside a Travel Air biplane easily identified by its rabbit-ear ailerons. From there stretched a row of radial-engined ghosts with ancient names: Waco, Fairchild, and Stearman. Beyond them like Christmas presents too big to fit beneath the tree, were Cubs, Porterfields, and Aeroncas, plus Luscombes, Funks and Taylorcrafts—all there for the Antique Airplane Association's annual Labor Day Reunion at Antique Airfield (IA27) near a little Iowa town called Blakesburg. It's located just north of the Missouri border and decades inside aviation's collective memories.

We slid onto the downwind leg to follow a Fleet biplane crawling on final approach as though unsure whether to land or hover. The air traffic controller standing beside the threshold waved his green flag at the arrival, and as it touched a red flag warned us: 'Don't land just yet.' We s-turned until the biplane ahead cleared, and the controller changed red to green before sitting back again on his lounge chair beside the tower chief, an antiquer who'd been safely directing Blakesburg's air traffic without any FAA interference for years. There is no real control tower or CTAF because few here use radios; no instrument approaches, just old airplanes with bellies oil-streaked to their tailwheels trailing in the sod, and pilots flying the way the gods intended flight with stick and rudder.

With that barnstormer image etched in my head, I slipped the Marquart Charger biplane wing-low toward the end of the runway just beyond the hickory trees. A gentle crosswind tried to drift my world sideways, but the biplane seemed to find the slot without me and was about to flare just above the grass when, so proud of myself was I, that I mentally patted myself on the back and felt the walloping thwack of the gear hitting earth, a reminder that heroes land well, while amateurs merely arrive.

Bounce, float, and another little bounce in case any of the hundreds of spectators didn't catch the first one, and we rolled toward the wire fence at the runway's end. Watching dogs scatter and mothers grab their children, I knew my arrival had impressed the crowd as thoroughly as it no-doubt wowed my wife in the front cockpit, who until recently thought flying a little dangerous. Still we were down, and I taxied to a row of other biplanes in a section reserved for Second Generation Antiques, the newest class of aging airplanes in the club.

New Antiques?

My 180-hp Marquart Charger MA-5 was built—thankfully not by me—almost 30 years after Robert Taylor created the Antique Airplane Association in 1953. Talk about vision; back then, Lindbergh's Spirit of St. Louis was only 26 years old—younger than much of today's rental fleet. A good portion of the airplanes now considered antiques hadn't even been riveted when Taylor saw the need to preserve what was yet to come. Imagine forming an Antique Cirrus Association in 2005.

But Taylor and a handful of pilots and mechanics dedicated to preserving what they knew to be tomorrow's classics secured my future. So, today, I get to fly open-cockpit biplanes cross-country, head-in-the clouds and sometimes in my own ego when landing before large crowds. It's heaven, and, yes, it's in Iowa.

The greatest part of flying an open-cockpit biplane is the arrival factor. I pulled to a stop and swung the tail in a swirl of grass clippings and empty lawn chairs. Hats flew in the prop blast, as campers in a nearby tent pulled on clothes and shook fists as I killed the engine. Then, I slipped off my harness straps, and like Eddie Rickenbacker returning from the *Meuse-Fromage* front after bagging a brace of Fokker D-7s, I gripped the upper wing handles, stood in the seat, and swung one and then the other foot over the cockpit and onto what I thought was the lower wing's walkway only to catch my sneaker in flying wires and tumble toward the ground while still wearing my cloth helmet, which—since its headset cord was still plugged in—ripped away from my ears and slammed against the fuselage in a humiliating thump.

"I give your landing a four," Brent Taylor, Bob's son and Director of the Air Power Museum, greeted us, "But you lose points for the dismount." With that, we'd arrived. But, hey, if you can't humiliate yourself around family, where else, then? And the Antique Airfield is all about family.

It ain't Oshkosh. It's smaller on the order of magnitude that a Jaguar is less than the Queen Mary. One has subtle class, the other packs in a big crowd. The Blakesburg family is relatively small and highly selective. It's only open to anyone who longs to "Keep The Antiques Flying." Over the Labor Day weekend pilots from the four corners of the nation converged to share this unique experience, to sleep beneath wings, hand-prop Cubs, and debrief in the on-field Pilot's Pub where stories can't be told without spilling beer as you describe your loop to a snap to a falling leaf in the Bucker biplane of your dreams.

Antiques in the proper minds aren't merely old airplanes that look pretty on display. Instead, they're time machines—a weave of struts and flying wires designed in the 1920s and flown into the future. The antiquer with joystick in one hand and throttle in the other doesn't operate inside Class G-or-whatever airspace but, instead, climbs into a 1929 sky to barnstorm with Jake Hollow and Kate Strauss or to drift lazily across the ripe corn in a J-3 Cub with the doors open taking in a 1946 sunset. To the antiquer flying behind a radial engine, the clock turns backwards above the X that marks a spot in the universe, where if you don't believe in time, your spirit flies forever.

© 2005

Chapter 9
Defiance

"Someone"

In the dream someone shook the cracking branch where David perched inches above molten lava flows. "Get your shoes on," a woman's voice warned, which, given the deadly goo below, seemed pointless. Then his eyes popped open, and facing the bedroom window David saw a fiery glow just beyond the trees. The sky above pulsed red and yellow, highlighting the smoke that twisted on devilish thermals into the night.

"It's the airport," Caroline said, and by then Dave was fully awake but trying not to comprehend, wishing it were still a dream. Caroline pulled a sweatshirt over her head and ran from the room. "I'll get the truck!"

On any spring morning it's a sweet five-minute drive from their house to the airfield where two rows of faithful hangars always wait. For twenty-five years they'd taken that drive along the gravel road and into the parking lot separated from the flight line by a sign that reads: Pilots and Dreamers Welcome Beyond This Point. No Whining Allowed!

Dawn is usually the perfect time to be at the airport. Dew soaks your sneakers walking along the grass runway. Redwing blackbirds flit and shout avian curses from the cattails swaying in the ditches. A sparrow hawk often perches atop the windsock, scanning the fencerow for breakfast, which is always served fresh.

On this dawn flames slapped the sides of the two nearest hangars upstaging the sun's entrance. Metal siding crumpled, leaving the skeletal frame writhing in heat. There was plenty of evil light to watch the tortured end of a Cessna Birddog and a Citabria—trapped, dying, if not dead.

By then Dave and Caroline were running along the hangar row. More cars arrived, and half-dressed pilots scrambled out, each sprinting in orange anxiety toward hangars either in flames or threatened. "Forget that one!" a dark figure shouted. "Too hot; go to the next hangar and bust open the door!" Everyone ducked when a Cherokee's fuel tank exploded inside the hangar that was "too hot." Sirens called in the distance, but it was obvious they were many impossible minutes away to help. "Phwoomph!" Another fuel tank blew, and another hangar collapsed taking its Stinson 108 with it.

No one noticed the real dawn's arrival. By the time the sun cleared the horizon there were fewer hangar shadows to paint across the ground. David and Caroline stood red-faced beside their Piper Pacer and a half-dozen other airplanes shoved as far from the flames as possible. These were the lucky ones. Elsewhere, pilots stared dumbfounded at what had been dream castles, now charred sticks and blackened skin.

Maybe someone cried and, perhaps, someone else swore at the biting smoke in her eyes. But by sunset, as hangar ruins smoldered beside ones left untouched, someone opened a cooler full of beer. Someone else pulled a sooty lawn chair from a scorched shed. And everyone smiled when the sparrow hawk slipped across the soft purple sky to perch atop the windsock and watch the rebuild begin.

© 2012

"An Untimely Decision"

Wedged between red canyon walls beneath lowering clouds, Cyrus first heard the voice. Distant, like a shaman's prayer in a cheap western movie, it rolled from the overhanging vapor and into his airplane. There, it harmonized with the engine's pulse until each piston stroke eerily slowed to match his drumming heartbeat. To handle the swelling fear his mind slowed time in order to delay the inevitable payment due for his decision to enter the canyon.

It hadn't seemed like a dumb choice. The dry riverbed appeared so inviting on the eastern side of the mountain where a wide tongue of alluvial sand lured him into the hills. For days Cyrus had been flying his Husky through the high country. He'd depart at dawn when the air was cool and land beside some creek before noon to sit out the heat. Later, he'd break camp and fly toward the evening thunderstorms roosting along the ridgelines. Dancing on nearby thermals he'd marvel at the curtains of rain that draped across the dry earth before vanishing into...

"Into what?" Cyrus asked himself, because he flew alone with no destination in mind. "How can a thunderstorm—or anything—simply vanish?" he questioned the virga as it did just that. And receiving no answer, he pressed into this canyon under a cloud that mocked time when it refused to vanish.

Flat riverbed turned to jagged rock where the canyon narrowed through a hallway of blind mirrors. Gone were the wide stretches of sand on which to land and await deliverance. His options ticked away to nothing when, there, in a shaft of sunlight poking through the gloom Cyrus saw his airplane's silhouette against the rocks. The stranger's voice chanted louder, still in beat with the engine. His hand shook on the joystick, and he squeezed the throttle as though to strangle the sound. Time had completely vanished, crushed in a vice between rock and cloud. There was no tomorrow or yesterday for Cyrus. His watch, if he'd looked, would display dead hands. He knew that time couldn't compete against stonewalls and thunder.

And that's when he looked toward his airplane's shadow and in that timeless moment saw it bank away. Its dusky pilot waved for him to follow. Cyrus chased his shadow down corridors where he couldn't see more than a few hundred yards and beneath ledges where lost Shoshone spirits chanted the song inside his engine and heart. And as the storm finally broke into pure energy, time sputtered back to life. The engine screamed as Cyrus desperately tried to fly for what he accepted to be his last seconds of earth life, when, suddenly, he burst into light above a wide expanse of sand.

Cyrus could never explain how he'd landed or how long he'd slept inside the airplane. But when he awoke the voice was gone, and through the skylight, all of the stars in the black sky grinned at him. And that's when he decided he could never fly alone again.

© 2008

"Toto's Revenge"

Best FBO? Hard to say. I'm no fan of metropolitan airports with their Berlin Wall security and prefer, instead, the outback fields where crop dusters fly 200-foot traffic patterns and tick-pimpled dogs sleep beside a broken pop machine with a sign that reads: "Leave money in coffee can. Signed, Betty."

Million Air at Van Nuys (VNY), California surprised me when I'd expected big-city snubs only to be treated like a fat-dollar celebrity. (Some say I'm easily mistaken for Robin Williams before liposuction, so maybe that was it.) Ramp fees were waived after I purchased a paltry ten gallons and swiped the last brownie off the counter.

Guymon (GUY) located in the accusing finger of Oklahoma's panhandle is an unsung bargain close to a great Mexican diner, and if you behave yourself at Frasca Field (C16) in Urbana, Illinois, you can tour Frasca's simulator factory. Show a respectful blend of awe and gratitude, and you may get the VIP trip through Rudy Frasca's private museum of war birds, old birds, and odd birds. Don't touch anything.

Flower Aviation in Salina, Kansas (SLN) makes any tramp pilot's Top Ten list. And it's not just because of the pretty girls in tight shorts who direct transients into tie-down spots and then cause middle-aged men to drop jaw-first from their airplanes watching them bend over to chock the tires.

Okay, that might be one of the reasons. The other is the lobby where you'll eat fresh chocolate-chip cookies and get sworn at by a parrot, macaw, or whatever that foul-speaking thing is that was obviously raised by Navy linguists.

Kansas, parked midway between everything hip on the West Coast and urbane on the East, needs to do something to get noticed. Cookies alone won't do it, so the state offers a bigger show as I relearned when wandering through on no particular route in something unsophisticated that taxis with its tail in the dirt and no lid over the cockpits. Four wings completed my barnstorming ensemble, so wherever I'd arrive someone usually remarked, "Nice biplane; think you'll ever learn to land it?" At least in Salina they smile when they say that—giggle, actually.

For those unfamiliar with the Midwest, here's a quick lesson: It's not all flat. Iowa even has ski resorts, although, they are a bit silly; my favorite is located near the Boone (BNW) airport, where there's a homebuilders' workshop/co-op open to anyone having trouble riveting together a quick-build RV-8.

Kansas, however, is a flat billiard table stretching to all horizons covered in endless pastures and whatever it is growing below in waving green felt. In the cool morning sky a few hundred feet above all that waving, I could see as far as the earth's curvature allowed. Beyond that I didn't care, because the openness sucked my mind dry, removing all remnants of 1970s Rocky Mountain highs and filled the void with a 2-D vision that staggers most viewers but made me want to fly above it forever. Or at least until the afternoon sky warmed and all that green below sweated into the air currents rising to colder heights. Plus, I was hungry and almost out of gas, so taking a tip from a freight dog who knew where to find free cookies, I headed to Salina.

The tower controller wasn't particularly friendly, and to punctuate my disdain for his indifference, I demonstrated a triple-bounce wheel landing on the 12,000-foot runway.

"If able, turn left at the end," he said, "And taxi to the ramp."

I was able and did, following a shorts-clad ramp rat waving parking batons like a KU cheerleader. I think his name was Daryl, and it was apparent that he handled the lesser customers while the biz jet behind me received the full Flower reception.

Still, like Odysseus on the Isle of Babes I lingered until the weather soured. Flight Service painted an optimistic picture of the route: "If you hurry and get real lucky, you may survive the line of Level Unbelievable thunderstorms forming between Salina and Topeka." Once in Topeka (TOP) the forecast called for clear skies and sweet siren songs all the way to my final resting place, er, destination in Iowa. So, I departed and, like Odysseus, I must've irritated the weather gods, and because I didn't understand that Kansas could morph into a mountain state I found myself weaving through canyons of vertical development the likes of which gives any sensible barnstormer pause. Unfortunately, every airport where I'd hoped to pause went down the weather toilet.

Smart pilots avoid anything made of water vapor the color of marshmallows growing to 70,000 feet. It was late afternoon, and Kansas having broiled all day in the sun now released its steamed energy skyward. The air was deceptively smooth at the feet of these towering thugs, but as I tuned nearby AWOS frequencies, reports deteriorated from rain, to wind, to blowing frogs.

I monitored Flight Watch (122.0) with the thought of climbing on top, but heard an anxious Bonanza driver several thousand feet above me trying to make the same mistakes only to report that the clouds grew around him so fast that he turned tail for Texas. I decided to do likewise back to Salina only to find my back door closed. Cut off, my plans shifted from reaching Topeka to considering a survivable side road landing.

The gods toy with the wayfarer who ignores evidence of his own stupidity. So as clouds boiled around me in unbelievable glory and terror, thumping their vaporous chests, I pressed eastward through a twisting alleyway of narrowing sanity above Kansas' greenery, and running just a little faster than the squall line, floated into Topeka. No cookies, no bargain-priced avgas or Playmate staff, just a guy in a blue work shirt leaning into the wind to help me tie the biplane down shortly before the sky unloaded.

Best FBO? Tough to say, but as lightning chiseled the sky, I was damn glad this one was there.

© 2005

"Gorged"

In wing shade beneath a clear sky at Pendleton, Oregon we waited for a thunderstorm the size of a vertical Rhode Island to quit the Cascade Mountains. It seemed to regenerate itself by sucking energy from some dormant volcano, and we couldn't take the Columbia River Gorge until it lifted the cumulus gate. By late afternoon the storm quit thumping its chest, stepped off the mountain and walked away to die alone in the prairie.

"Follow us," a Skywagon pilot called as we scrambled to our airplanes like RAF pilots eager to chase away Heinkels. "Fly low beneath the clouds, and when you enter the Gorge keep to the right. There's not much room, and you don't wanna hit someone comin' the other way."

"You serious?" I squeaked.

His mad grin said that he was. "Do it all the time! Piece of…" and the last word vanished in the wind. With my first Pacific Northwest briefing completed I followed the leader to the runway. At first it was easy; disaster entry usually is. But as we intercepted the river and headed west I lost the pack. They were fast. I was slow. They knew the terrain. I didn't know squat but continued, too embarrassed to admit defeat. Somewhere past The Dalles I poked my nose into the Gorge with all the confidence of a minnow sticking its head into an eel's mouth. Fat-bottomed clouds sagged a low overcast and draped like theater curtains down sheer rock on either side. I wondered what a cow might think while pointed down a slaughterhouse chute.

And that's when I heard the sound. A thin, tapering hiss, I dismissed it as something dying inside the engine—a spun bearing perhaps or disintegrating piston rings. Engine failure above the Columbia River's white caps withered in comparison with the thought of rounding the bend ahead after which there was no turning back.

The hiss turned to a screech as I cautiously swiveled to stare at the canyon constricted by fluff that pulled me deeper. Picture a freeway through a mountain pass—first eight lanes, then four as it pinches further between padded cliffs. Now imagine that road turning blindly in the semidarkness of roiling vapor, inviting the adventurous or, in my case, the bonehead stupid to simply follow the path to….

To what? "Follow us," the ghost rider had called. He'd flown this route his whole life, knew every dam, curve, and power line. I suddenly understood with bovine clarity how little I knew, and the sound screaming in my ears was my own voice: "Noooo….!"

It rained that night at Hood River airport, fifty miles short of Portland. I listened to the drops tap on aluminum skin, and falling asleep inside the fuselage I thought: "Can't ever admit I chickened out…but, then again, I'd hate to say that I pressed on merely because a stranger had ordered me to follow. At dawn I bowed to a clear sky and followed no one to my runway.

© 2006

"Waco 10"

It was a 1928 Waco 10 biplane from the Golden Age of Grace and Beauty that existed before airplanes had distracting add-ons such as doors, cabin heat and starters. Deep burgundy with silver doped wings; it looked like a barnstormer momentarily paused on the ramp at Osceola, Iowa. Once fueled, it would lift off again and return to 1928 to complete its ride-giving circuit before the winter snows chased it south.

I taxied the Citabria to the fuel pumps and felt my airplane gaze respectfully at the old dowager. Somehow in a hidden realm visited only by airplanes, they communicated, and the Citabria no doubt saluted.

There were two airplanes waiting—the Waco and a light blue Baby Ace. They'd been to Brodhead, Wisconsin and were on the last leg home to Creston, Iowa. Tanks topped off, bills paid, the Baby Ace pilot swung her leg over the Waco's rear cockpit lip and settled into the seat to help her husband start the OX-5.

"Switch off," he called from the propeller.

"Switch off," she answered.

The pilot pulled the curvaceous wooden propeller through, and the OX-5 engine clacked softly. "Make it hot," he said.

"Switch hot," she answered.

He swung the propeller like someone trying to move an elephant by tugging at its trunk and with about the same result—nothing happened.

"Switch off," he called.

"Switch off," she answered.

He pulled the prop through another blade. "Hot."

"Hot."

He swung it again and, again, nothing happened.

"Off."

"Off."

I climbed the ladder to fuel the Citabria, and as 100 octane fumes floated up, I watched the Waco couple.

"Hot."

"Hot."

Swing. Nothing.

"Off."

"Off."

Reset.

"Hot."

"Hot."

I continued to watch from inside the FBO, and, as I walked back after stopping to thumb through a three-month-old Trade-A-Plane, I passed the Waco people—the man leaning against a lower wing, exhausted, staring at the OX-5 as though waiting for the spark of divine inspiration. The pilot in the rear cockpit offered no advice. There was a stillness about the scene that indicated that Wacos start when Wacos want to start and humans have only to wait.

While I drained a sample of fuel from the Citabria the Waco couple continued their "Hot-Off-Hot-Off..." ritual. I climbed inside the cockpit and as unobtrusively as possible—skipping the usual "Clear prop" call for fear of insulting them—I flipped the master, set the mags, and pressed the starter button. Embarrassed, I quickly throttled back to idle when the Lycoming O-320 barked to life as it always does.

I taxied away not wanting to make eye contact. But turning onto the runway I looked as they resumed their start procedure, and before I advanced the throttle I could only envy them—not the fact that they'd be hand-propping until next spring, but, instead, I envied the beauty of two people caught up in a ritual dating back to that era of grace and beauty—an era that longed for the future of self-starters.

© 2002

"Stall Recovery"

Kate set the empty coffee pot back on the hotplate and poured the last glub of cream for the cat asleep on a Final Notice for an unpaid fuel bill. He curled tighter, annoyed by human intrusion. Wind gently shook the window, and beyond the glass a biplane rocked its wings like the outstretched arms of a floating corpse. Since the Travel Air had burned its last gallon of Sinclair HC it sat grounded and with it, Kate thought, her life.

Nineteen thirty-three had been an awful year for Katharine Marie Strauss who'd been trying, against her ex-husband's advice, to earn a living in aviation. Twenty-eight and '29 had been good, '30 not so bad, but by late 1931 her dreams for High Plains Aero Service staggered with each economic blow. While Roosevelt promised happy days again, Kate sold all but one airplane and told pilots looking for work to keep moving, sorry, no jobs, but help yourself to the bunk inside the hangar. Eventually, even they disappeared, and, now, as Kate stepped outside and pulled her leather jacket against the approaching winter she felt hollow. Wind hummed through the biplane's flying wires and tugged at the canvas tarp wrapped around the Wright J-4 radial engine. A sparrow landed on the tail and looked over the biplane as though considering it for a winter home. Unimpressed, it lifted and vanished in a gust. Kate wondered if that would be her last customer.

Summer had been dry, autumn without harvest. Customers no longer lined up on Saturday mornings waiting for airplane rides across the prairie and along the river. She recalled evenings when she'd drop from the cockpit exhausted after a full day hauling passengers. The gas boy would climb to the top wing lugging the hose over his shoulder, and with fumes and gnats circling his red hair, he'd

140

call: "Not a bad day; we'll do even better tomorrow." And the tomorrows got better until they, too, dried up.

Kate swept her hand along a lower wing to flick away last summer's bugs and looked up toward the distant murmur of round engines. A United Airlines Boeing 247 on its daily run from Chicago, droned overhead headed to the capital airport. She'd never flown a transport but knew she could, and wouldn't it be something to have a flying job that could never disappear?

She stepped onto the Travel Air's lower wing, uncovered the rear cockpit and as though climbing into bed slipped her legs over its rim. The familiar smell of burnt motor oil on doped cotton—like fried bananas—swept away thoughts of real jobs, and she gently squeezed the throttle to the cold engine. Her right hand pulled the joystick back as though climbing toward the sky she couldn't afford. But before pity could kill the lift inside her she nudged the stick forward, because the thing that made Kate fly refused to stall. And despite the rest of the world's reality she knew they'd fly again.

© 1989

"The Art Critic"

Late afternoon sunlight made the FAA inspector squint as he stopped his G-car in front of Hal's hangar. Carl "Smile 'n File" Hammer opened the door and stepped into a puddle. He stopped smiling long enough to wipe mud from his shoe on the black wall tires. Hal barely glanced at him from beneath his 1946 Taylorcraft but snickered just a little.

"Aren't doin' your own maintenance again, are ya, Hal?" Carl asked as he entered the hangar uninvited.

"Wouldn't think of it," Hal answered the way you'd answer a cop who asks if you were speeding…when you were. "All the bars closed today?" Hal didn't expect an answer and slid further down the airplane's belly, touching a brush to the fabric. Carl squatted.

"Painting the fuselage brown?" Meaning, that's an ugly choice.

"Some TSA regulation against it?" Hal replied. Carl shrugged and stood. "No, but word has it you've been flying…"

"More than fifty years," Hal interrupted through teeth clenching an unlit pipe. "Feds just notice?"

"You know what I mean," Carl sighed. "You lost your medical…" And before Hal could protest Carl waved his hand, adding, "You can't fly solo under sport pilot once your medical's been pulled. So, until you get cleared, you need someone to act as PIC—Pilot-in-Command…"

"I know what it means," Hal growled to cover the hurt, not from the recent bypass surgery but from the way his life was being taken from him. His breathing body was rapidly losing its soul. To survive he'd sneak aloft periodically and motor into a sunrise, careful to land again before the wrong eyes noticed.

Hal was an aerial artist who'd flown a lifetime across his favorite canvas—the sky. Flight wasn't transportation to him. He'd never used a GPS and wasn't impressed with anyone's glass panel. His spirit lived alone above the planet, and, now, he was told he'd have to leave it there. Most on the airfield were surprised to see how meekly he took the grounding. Fewer noticed that he'd begun to repaint the airplane.

It was almost sunset when Hal rolled the T-craft from the hangar and maneuvered what appeared to be a scarecrow into the left seat. Made from mechanics overalls stuffed with old Pacific Flyer pages, its head was a balloon painted with a smiling face and PIC printed across the forehead. Hal set the mag switch on, throttle at idle and hand-spun the propeller. His shaggy gray hair whipped in the slipstream as he climbed inside and spotted Carl leaning on the fence.

No one's sure what Carl saw. But once Hal was airborne we saw that his airplane resembled a giant paintbrush. The fuselage was brown, and the yellow wings were etched with countless black lines like bristles. And then, Hal, the aerial artist, defied the critics and painted his heart across the horizon.

Back at the hangar was a note from Carl: "Art is anything you can get away with, and you got away with a masterpiece."

© 2009

"Red Menace"

She had red hair. He had blond. Her biplane wore red skin, his yellow. The sunrise over Paniola Bay that February morning was volcanic amber, and Gene knew she'd be hiding in the fireball waiting to pounce. Holding his thumb toward the sun to block its rays he looked for her silhouette in the surrounding glare, a trick he'd learned from watching Black Sheep Squadron reruns. Still no sign of her.

Gene banked his Pitts hard left and then right. The wingtips sliced the Hawaiian sky, sectioning the mountains and ocean into neat boxes, each a possible threat. He twisted his neck and pushed his goggles onto his forehead for a clearer view. She might be lurking in the cumulus clouds forming atop the ridgeline, but it was too early in the day to provide much cover. No, she'd be in the sun's glare — a cat to his mongoose. So he continued to climb and sensing her presence he lowered his goggles before reaching for the gun's charging handle.

It was a single lever mounted between the cabane struts. He pulled hard. Engine and wind noise around the open cockpit blocked the sound, but he felt the valve open to the compressed gas cylinder strapped to the floorboards. He glanced at the gun mounted atop the upper wing with its barrel set to fire over the propeller's arc. He knew he shouldn't waste rounds but flipped up the safety cover over the fire button on the joystick and touched off a short burst.

A half-dozen .68 caliber rounds vanished into the sky. The muzzle velocity was so slow that Gene wondered if it were possible to catch his own rounds. Still, he'd been paintball dogfighting for almost a year and knew that in the right attack posture he could best his instructor. If only he could find her first.

Splat! Splat! Splat! His musings were shredded by green latex rounds splattering against the windscreen, cockpit rim and turtle deck behind his head. And her shadow flashed across his face before he could react. Right

Despite knowing he was dead Gene chopped power, kicked rudder and tucked into a sloppy hammerhead trying to get on her tail. But too late. With the sun now uselessly behind him he watched his wife inscribe a slow victory roll across the sky, throw on smoke and descend toward their private airfield. Gene followed her down and before he touched he could see her climbing from the cockpit. When she removed her helmet the red hair only made her smile glow brighter, and he had to acknowledge defeat as he taxied alongside.

"Happy Valentine Day," she called, and he felt the biplane rock when she placed her foot on the lower wing. "You cheat," he grumbled. She laughed, kissed him lightly where green paint stuck to

his cheek and whispered, "All's fair in love, dogfights and paintball."
And minutes later as the two biplanes spiral-climbed over the ocean
she sensed he wouldn't play fair anymore.

© 2012

"Old Gray"

Dawn slipped over the mountains and quietly extinguished the
desert stars in passing. They didn't seem to mind. Having kept watch
all night it was time, again, for sunlight to rouse earth dwellers from
bed. Chuck dwelled above the planet so was already awake and at the
airport. After parking his Studebaker Lark he kicked the hangar door
to chase out any snakes that might've curled beneath the rubber skirt.
When nothing stirred, he slid the door open and smiled at the old Tri-
Pacer waiting beneath a dusty skylight. She smiled back.

Painted the same light gray of his mothballed West Point
uniform, she had pearl white wings trimmed in blue. Piper chevrons
raked her tail. She looked as though she'd been awake all night
combing the stars for dreams. And, maybe, caught a few. Chuck
walked around the nose and patted her cowling. If Piper made Tri-
Pacer biscuits he would've fed her one. And, yes—he'd tell anyone
who didn't understand—the Tripe was a she. Chuck didn't give a rat's
butt who thought it inappropriate to think of his old gray beauty as
female. Something this pretty couldn't be otherwise. And he'd stare
down anyone who claimed that Tri-Pacers were funny looking. Those
same fools turned up their noses at Navions and Apaches.

With one hand on the strut, Chuck ducked beneath the right wing
to open the cockpit door. Leaning inside, he inhaled that elegant blend
of leather and butyrate dope with a hint of avgas. He wondered why it
couldn't be bottled so all women could smell as good: *Eau d'Avion*—
$1000 per ounce. Chuck was a romantic and a causeless rebel who
couldn't explain his attachment to this airplane. She wasn't as sleek as
those Mooneys that taxied by with their tails on backwards. Nor could
she haul the load of a rumbling Skylane. "But so what?" he asked
aloud. "I love her." But mostly he loved the thought of her in flight.

Outside in the cool air with the throttle set, Chuck reached
beneath the seat for the starter button. "TSA couldn't confiscate you if
they wanted," he muttered. "They couldn't find your starter with both
hands." The white hair on his neck bristled thinking of the country's

worst agency. He shook it off and looked toward the pink desert sky. And by the time they departed all thoughts of fools flushed from his mind, replaced by airplane dreams coming to life.

It was their daily routine. Together, they'd wander about the morning sky, the short-winged Piper telling Chuck what she knew about flight. Despite their long relationship, each trip offered new insights into life beyond gravity. And returning to land, he'd let his companion find her way to the runway as she had for over 50 years. There was nothing he could teach her. She wouldn't listen if he'd tried. And, later, he'd thank her for the visit while yearning for the next dawn when she'd reveal more dreams taken from the desert stars.

© 2009

"Right of the People"

They gathered in a circle beneath the hangar's dusty shop lamp. Shadows forced Curtis to shift to keep the newspaper in the light. "Read it again," someone asked in a soft voice. Curtis cleared his throat before reading the newly ratified amendment to the Constitution: "A well regulated Sky, being necessary to the security of a free State, the right of the people to keep and fly Aircraft, shall not be infringed."

"Man, that's good," Jean muttered. "And all in one sentence. Did you notice? That's good writing. How many words in it?"

Curtis counted and answered, "Twenty-seven." And they all stood quietly considering the impact of those few words that seemed to guarantee their right—not merely a privilege—to fly.

"Shall not be infringed," Chuck repeated. His voice rolled up from some deep recess, gaining power as it left his mouth. "That means we—the People—got the right to fly, and no one, not even TSA, can take it away; 'bout damn time, too." And most of the crowd mumbled agreement, except Thomas who frowned and asked to see the paper. He read it slowly to himself before saying, "This first part concerns me." He tapped the paper with a finger. "The way it starts, 'A well regulated Sky, being necessary to the security of a free State...'"

"So what?" Chuck interrupted. "Makes sense to have some rules, like we already got for IFR, VFR, right-of-way and such..."

"Just concerns me," Thomas hesitated. "Like, maybe, the government might point to the 'well-regulated' part whenever it wants to clamp down…"

"Shall not be infringed," Chuck struck back. "That means we fly what we own, and they got nothin' to say about it!" The vehemence with which he defended the phrase masked an unspoken fear.

Thomas shook his head. "Remember when TSA made us all get these silly badges just to get to our own hangars?" He flicked the tag clipped to his overalls. "They decide what's well regulated."

Chuck slowly unclipped his security badge, smiled and tossed it to the floor. The others stood in awe witnessing what they knew was an FAR violation. Chuck drew up his full six-foot-two-inch height and ground the offending badge beneath his boot heel.

Jean was next, and after she flung her security badge to the oily pavement the other pilots threw theirs into a loose pile. Only Thomas remained still wearing his badge. The clack of an air compressor kicking on covered an uncomfortable silence. But by the time it quit Thomas had gathered the badges and, adding his own, dropped them into a trashcan. Once outside the hangar with the aerodrome beacon flashing overhead, he drizzled avgas over them. And then, before dropping a lit match, he intoned, "Shall not be infringed!"

It'd be left to future generations of pilots to decide if it was the Constitutional amendment or the People's interpretation that saved aviation. But on that July 4th evening a handful of rebel pilots declared independence from tyranny.

© 2009

"Launch the Revolution"

By afternoon the crowd had grown to several thousand around the airport's perimeter. Faces turned skyward with eyes shaded against the sun when an official worried, "He refuses to come down."

Even the guards in the tower protected by concertina wire gazed at the small airplane overhead, unsure what to do. The tower chief ran up the stairs, her footsteps clanging against steel. Breathless, she demanded binoculars although it was clear she'd never see the truth. "How long has that been up there?"

"Ten hours," a tower guard answered through a smile. "Maybe twelve."

"That's impossible."

"So we thought," he replied and then indicated the crowd below. "But word spread. This morning it was just a few. Now look at the cars coming from all directions." Indeed, the roads were packed. More people arrived on bicycles and some on foot to see the man who flew without permission, refusing to come down.

Disgusted, the tower chief pressed the binoculars at the guard and demanded, "Have you ordered him down?" And before he could reply the crowd murmured as the tiny airplane, little more than a butterfly with yellow wings and a green tail, lowered its nose. "What's he doing?"

"A loop, I think...Yup, it's a loop."

"Well, stop him, make him stop that illicit looping!"

The crowd applauded as the little airplane traced a perfect O. And in one voice they gasped when the airplane pulled into what appeared to be another loop but at the top did not dive. Instead, it hung in the air, its silver propeller slicing the blue. Its wings slowly rotated from the torque until they realized they could no longer lift and dropped into a spin. In turn after turn the airplane spun toward the earth. And then as crash trucks lurched and eyes peered between fingers, it climbed again bringing a shout from the crowd.

"I'll take his license!" the tower chief spat.

"You've already taken all the licenses," the guard noted. "Nothing left to take." And he, too, silently cheered the pilot.

"That's...that's nonsense!"

"Isn't it, though," the guard laughed and then pointed toward the hangars where more pilots—without authorization—smashed locks and pushed little airplanes into the sunlight. The tower chief grabbed a microphone and tried to restore order, but her mouth only flapped like a bass sucking air in a fisherman's net. Powerless, she watched engines start, and without any regard for her authority dozens of little airplanes taxied to the runway. She managed a gagging plea to "Stop..." but stared in disbelief at those who escaped her grasp and lifted into what she'd presumed was her sky, a sky to be jealously controlled.

Slumping into administrative oblivion she vanished amid the sound of airplanes twirling about her head. Soon the guards abandoned the tower to join the mob as it swarmed over the fence and spread blankets on the grass. And long past sunset they watched the power of lift wielded by revolutionaries who refused to come down.

© 2006

"First Flight Deserved Last Rites"

Dreamers by definition live on the edge of reality and learn that to deviate from the sublime can lead to unintended enlightenment. In the summer of 1967, my aviation fantasies reformed when I took my first airplane ride.

A Civil Air Patrol (CAP) recruiter promised flight that I, a 13-year-old dreamer, expanded into visions of being at the controls of a T-38 jet trainer, taxiing to the runway with the canopy up and an oxygen mask dangling from my helmet. I envisioned smooth climbs past marshmallow clouds where I'd impress the instructor with loops and rolls and perhaps a maneuver that the Air Force hadn't yet imagined. So, it was with profound anticipation that I stood in formation at McGuire Air Force Base in New Jersey with several thousand other sweating CAP cadets, our acned faces scarlet from the heat. A colonel resembling Ernest Borgnine wiped his forehead and gave the vital preflight mission briefing: "The first flight commences after lunch, so don't eat too much." That was it; not a lot of info for a first-time flyer, but being a teenager, I ignored what I didn't understand and packed away macaroni salad, tater tots, and lime Jell-O, washed down with a half-gallon of chocolate milk.

Later, outside the mess hall we loaded onto blue school buses and rode to the flight line where instead of rows of sleek T-38s we found a lone—rather worn—C-130 Hercules, four-engine transport shimmering in the dull heat, its back end open like a panting eel awaiting prey. A crewman, barely older than us, stood on the ramp smirking with bemused distain. Being a teenager, I was used to that look from adults but didn't expect it on my first flight.

"Find a seat and buckle in," he called as we herded into the Herc's belly. Intense heat sucked the air from my lungs, and I dropped onto a canvas seat along the bulkhead beneath a window that was too high above me to use. "Let's git a move on, gentlemen," our host grumbled. Then, as the ramp door shut he gave his welcome-aboard speech: "Don't touch nuthin', don't get out a' yer seats 'til I says so, and don't puke on my airplane." I vaguely wondered what he meant by that, because I felt fine. "If'n you do feel dis-com-fort," he continued, "then use the bags located above your seats." Then, he disappeared before I could ask him to repeat, since I didn't see any bags. Still, I wasn't ill, so I handled the information the way I did most adult advice and ignored it.

As yet, my first flight didn't match my soaring imagination. Where I'd expected fighter-style cockpits, I now sat strapped on a bench inside a solar oven with no view of the sky. An engine whined to life and managed to route its kerosene exhaust into the fuselage. Eventually, all four turbines churned against the heat, and we taxied for what seemed like miles, although without a window I could only mark progress as the wheels clicked across the joints in the pavement. The heat intensified and soon burnt jet fuel was all we breathed, but being from New Jersey my lungs could handle it.

Finally, this aluminum warehouse with its wilted cargo rumbled down the runway until with an upward pitch of the deck, followed moments later by the groan of gear retracting, I knew we were flying. Since entering the airplane however, I hadn't seen a speck of sky but despite this, I knew I'd crossed over from being a dreamer of flight to flyer.

"You can stand up and look outside now," the airman called. As one, we unbuckled our seatbelts, stood and lunged to peer through the few available windows. But as I stood and turned, I felt all the squishy parts inside my head continue to spin even though my skull had stopped. Instantly, as though I'd been injected with a fast-acting emetic, my skin chilled, knees unhooked, and I slid like wet laundry onto the seat and stared at the floor, where there appeared two well-shined black shoes beneath an airman's voice: "You ain't gonna puke now are you?"

I tried to answer, but, instead of words, macaroni salad and tater tots in a slurry of warm chocolate milk and lime Jell-O shot from my mouth and onto those shiny shoes.

There was much yelling after that, but I didn't care because I was dying. In all my earthbound fantasies of flight, I'd never once dreamt of airsickness, didn't know it existed, and I'd guess that any of the dozen or so other cadets on that flight who soon followed my lead to coat an Air Force transport's floor with barely-chewed mess hall chow, were equally surprised at this phenomenon.

After 20 minutes of shaking CAP cadets into jellied wretches above the New Jersey Pine Barrens in the summer heat, the C-130 returned to base. The landing gear moaned down and locked, before its tires smacked the runway with the grace of a cement truck dropped from a Zeppelin. And as we taxied back I expected to see a row of ambulances waiting to haul us to emergency Red Cross tents. But, instead, the Hercules stopped, dropped its back ramp, and with military efficiency we were herded off—green-faced and broken—while the next batch of cadets marched up the other side of the ramp, no-doubt wondering what fate awaited them aloft. I can still see their faces as the cargo door sealed them inside the fetid C-130's belly before it taxied away.

Some firsts aren't so hot. On that, my first flight, I didn't even get to look out the window. There was no joyous swooping and soaring. I didn't slip surly bonds or touch the face of anyone's god but, instead, merely heaved on an unsung airman's shoes, who, if you're reading this, "Sorry, but you should've know better."

Still, whatever dream had led me to flight, survived, despite this gut-shot of reality, and although it took several more flights—none in a C-130—before anyone would invite me back a second time, my dream of wings never died. And today when a new student climbs into the cockpit with me, I never mention the possibility of aerial dis-com-fort because I don't want to plant a bad seed inside a dreamer's imagination where fantasies of flight should grow. Enlightened as I now am, however, I won't hesitate to cinch a garbage bag over their heads at the first hint of a dream reaching the edge.

© 1986

"It's Over!"

A dead winter day in the mountains, and snow piled fast against the hangar. Inside, Hal smoked his pipe by the barrel stove while threading a strand of .032 safety wire through a tail wheel bolt. His '46 Taylorcraft looked over his shoulder like a horse watching a farrier shod its hoof. Smoke memories climbed past Hal's face and woolen cap atop curly gray hair. He strained through grimy reading glasses and swore gently when the wire poked his thumb. Blood reflected tiny images of his blue eyes before dripping to the floor.

"It's over!" a slender figure in white overalls called while waving a newspaper at him. It was silhouetted by sudden bright sunlight from an unseen window.

Hal turned. "Who are…What's over?"

"The Aviation Recession. It's officially over." The apparition floated into the hangar as though on air. "Says so here." It held the newspaper toward Hal who squinted at the headline: Aviation Foe Calls It Quits!

The visitor circled through Hal's hangar, stopping beneath a faded aircraft tool calendar. A bikini-clad Miss February leaned from the page to read the article. "Lemme see," she said and then read aloud: "Government declares general aviation to be the winner…."

"Winner in what?" Hal grumbled.

"In the war to keep free minds on the ground," she continued. "You've been inside this hangar too long, Hal. They've surrendered; you've won."

Hal stood, reached for the paper and reread the announcement. Setting it down he paused before removing his pipe from his mouth. When he tapped the bowl against the parts washer the messenger flinched watching the sparks bounce onto a pile of old rags.

"He does that a lot," Miss February whispered. "Surprised he hasn't burnt this old shack down years ago."

Without comment Hal slid the hangar door open and stepped into sunshine to gaze at unbound joy overtaking the airfield. Other hangar doors opened, freeing airplanes that hadn't seen light in years. The gas truck drove by with Avgas $0.65/Gallon freshly painted on the side. The FBO had a fleet of new Cessna 150s lined up for rent. And across from that were twice as many new Piper Cubs and Cherokees ready to launch. A large banner announced: Introductory Flight $5.

Snow melted off hangar roofs, and grass shoots pushed through runway cracks. Hal saw pilots rip the airport's security gate from its posts. As he approached, the crowd parted in respect for the oldest tenant on the field. There, an ashen-faced TSA agent solemnly removed epaulettes from her uniform, bowed to Hal and muttered, "I'm sorry. It was all a mistake. We surrender." Then she offered the once-dreaded symbols of abused power to the old flyer.

Hal turned and walked toward his hangar where Miss February had slipped off the calendar. She'd rolled his airplane into the daylight and waited in the passenger's seat—motor running. As Hal slid beside her he called back to the vanquished TSA official: "Hey, no hard feelings…but don't ever darken my dreams again."

© 2010

Chapter 10
Holiday Flights

"A Swift Resolution"

Many of us had never seen Gene's hangar door open. So, when Sal poked his head into the pilots lounge calling, "He's opening the hangar!" we poured onto the ramp like RAF pilots running for their Hurricanes. Winded—because we weren't used to running—we formed a semi-circle to watch Gene shove a door-half along its rusted tracks. "Like rolling the stone away from a grave," Ed said, and we nodded at the biblical reference. I couldn't identify the actual passage but sensed a miraculous event.

"Anyone ever seen it fly?" a woman asked from the back of the crowd. Most hadn't, except Chuck, who'd been a flight instructor on the field for longer than anyone could remember. He moved to open the other door while the rest of us stood like carnival goers outside a sideshow tent, waiting for a glimpse of the two-headed goat. Even as sunlight flooded the hangar's interior for the first time in years, it took a minute to identify the bare metal fuselage with low wings. Its yellow tail sat on the floor, and a blue nose bowl flashed a toothy grin.

"It's a Swift," Chuck quietly announced and then almost whispered, "Gene hasn't flown since he ground-looped it ten years ago. Didn't cause much damage, just spooked him a bit. I helped him put it away that day but never thought he'd take so long to fly again. Every year he makes a resolution to fly it, but every year it stays grounded."

Gene was an airport regular who kept to himself. He'd wave, slip inside the hangar and latch the door behind him before curious visitors could intrude. Music—big-band jazz mostly—muffled any work sounds, so there was no telling what, if any, progress was made. Whenever asked, "When ya gonna fly it, Gene," he'd smile and answer, "Next year...next year." Now, another "next year" had two weeks behind it when Gene asked, "Can someone give me a hand pushing it out?" Twenty hands reached for the Swift, but Gene stopped them with, "Please use a clean rag, so you don't leave fingerprints." And when the old two-seater rolled outside you had to squint against the sunlight reflected in the polished skin.

The preflight inspection seemed to take all afternoon, allowing time for the crowd to grow. As the sunlight brushed the bare treetops orange, Gene climbed up the wing and settled into the left seat. There he sat scanning the instruments and seeming to gather enough courage to say: "Chuck, you probably think I need a flight review."

Chuck stepped onto the wing saying, "Oh, I know you can fly," and dropping onto the right seat, he added, "But I'd sure like to see you keep at least one of your New Year's resolutions."

Later, as the Swift lifted from the runway and folded its gear legs, I looked back at Gene's empty hangar and felt as though more than a promise had been kept. Perhaps a life had been reborn.

© 2008

"Fun With Dick & Jeanne"

"At least it's not snowing," Dick said just before the first wet flake tapped his nose. He brushed it away and climbed into the Super Cub after scraping his boot against the tire. Muddy water puddled on the scuffed floorboards as he flopped onto the rear seat. The old cushion formed to his butt from years of familiarity. Jeanne took the front seat with far more grace.

While Dick fumbled for his seatbelt, Jeanne called, "Clear prop!" The starter bit into the engine, popping it to life after two blades. Dick noted how easily Jeanne moved the throttle, keeping the RPMs down. Other students seemed unable to detect an engine screaming near redline, but Dick watched the rear throttle ease back to near idle.

He didn't complain about the cold blast through the open clamshell doors. He knew that part of the thrill of flying with "the old man in the Cub" was leaving the door open. Students came for the tail wheel endorsement, but they returned for the view. He'd lost count of how many pilots he'd trained. Most were already licensed tri-gear pilots who hadn't yet learned what feet were for. A few hours taildragging in a crosswind brought all their limbs into concert with wind and spirit. Or at least that's how he liked to think of it. Some never truly got the hang of it, but that didn't matter. They still experienced the beauty of stick and rudder with the sky sifting through the cockpit. By late December that sky was freezing.

Jeanne taxied to the end of the grass runway and crossed the paved one where a twin turbine had just landed. It scrunched to a stop in a vicious howl of reversed props, swirling mist and kerosene exhaust. The Super Cub passed through its wake, and bounced again in the gopher ruts along the grass runway.

"Ready?" Jeanne barely turned her head.

"When you are," he answered.

"Door open or closed?"

Dick hesitated before answering, "Open, cold air's good for the soul." Jeanne smiled, turned back and opened the throttle. Dick's toes hovered lightly above the rudder pedals. His hands barely touched stick and throttle, ready to take over. But Jeanne was no beginner, and the Cub never needed much runway even when fully loaded. With the tail up, she squeezed back on the stick, and they flew.

Dick tucked his chin tighter into his parka, but the cold damp air gave no quarter. He watched Jeanne's ponytail tap about her shoulders in the wind and remembered how that had first attracted him to her so many years before. And, now, on this New Year's afternoon, when the rest of the world digested chicken wings and football, he warmed at the chance to freeze his butt off flying behind the woman he loved. But that didn't stop him from finally saying, "Okay, enough beauty. Shut the door and put on the heater." She smiled. And from 500 feet they watched the world turn white.

© 2009

"Twelfth Night"

The wrench striking the concrete floor rang boxing bell clear, signaling I'd lost that round. It ricocheted into a back flip while I squeezed my hand, staunching blood from the scuffed knuckles. It then took a second hop, dissipating energy in chattering skips until resting in a corner beneath the Bellanca Cruisair's tail. There it sat, reminding me how stupid I'd been for using a crescent instead of a socket.

Vega, the ancient hangar cat, twitched her ears but didn't move from her perch atop the horizontal stabilizer. Nor did she express any sympathy as I knelt before her, stretching to reach the errant tool. Blood speckled the hangar floor, and I dabbed at it with a shop rag before wrapping the rag around my hand. The cat stared through regal eyes, unmoved by my discomfort but irritated that I'd disturbed her nap.

"Why couldn't you be a dog?" I growled. Her eyes replied, "And why couldn't you be anywhere else?" She then slipped from the airplane's triple-finned tail and, defying the gravity that had claimed the wrench, floated onto a nearby shelf.

There's little that's colder than a hangar floor in winter. It sucks the heat from your body no matter how well you're padded in boots and overalls. My ungloved fingers, poking from the bloodied rag, found the wrench and tossed it onto the workbench. Then, if I'd had any sense I should've walked away until spring when the skies would once again be fit to fly. But I'd made a pledge—the same one I'd made each New Year—to fly every day after work no matter what. Last year's attempt stalled at eleven nights. If I could just get the Bellanca out, I'd beat that.

Vega had watched me break resolutions so often she'd lost faith. If, indeed, cats have any faith in humanity. So it was with competing measures of determination and cynicism that we played our roles. She knew I'd fail, while I was determined to prove her wrong. Although the snow sifting beneath the hangar door as the winch lifted it into the rafters favored Vega's jaded view.

"It's still VFR!" I called to her as I pulled on the prop only to feel the wheels rock against immovable chocks. "I'm going flying!" I shouted and kicked the chocks. The cat merely blinked the way bankers do when you explain you're broke and need a loan.

Outside, I glanced up before climbing inside the airplane. The sky was the texture of congealed Malt-O-Meal with snow crystals swirling around the runway lights that clicked on as sunlight vanished.

"Clear prop!" And I pressed the starter button only to hear the depressing clicks of an unmotivated solenoid announcing a dead battery. I paused in defeat to watch the snow blanket the windshield, unwilling to face Vega who I knew smirked inside the hangar. The wrench never moved, but the clear ringing inside my head confirmed that on this, the twelfth night, I'd lost the match.

©2012

"Valentine Day"

Nowhere is colder than Valentine, Nebraska in February. Not even Fairbanks, Alaska where Amy and her Cessna 170 were from. Valentine wasn't her destination, not even an alternate. But watching her suddenly ex-boyfriend, Ted (a sluggish non-pilot), climb into the town's only taxicab, she felt that it was where her life might take off. For the moment, though, she was alone.

Around her the Sand Hills rolled in frozen waves like glaciers that refused to leave the prairie. Grass stubble poked through the snow converting the wind into choral voices with no need for words. Amy kicked boot heel to toe coaxing circulation into her feet before walking back to her airplane. Cold didn't bother her any more than it did to shed the guy she'd met a year ago in Santa Cruz, a place too mellow for her imagination.

"Let's escape," she'd said when she felt California's perfect sky almost trick her into staying. Her Cessna had sat too long on the airport's tie-down ramp, a visitor wedged among moldering airplanes whose owners had forgotten how to put dreams to flight.

"Where to?" Ted had asked suspiciously.

"Anywhere," she'd replied. And after weeks of flowing behind low-pressure troughs and sleeping in FBO lounges Ted's earthbound soul flew dangerously close to enlightenment. So, in Valentine he panicked and retreated home to exist comfortably until the end of his time on a planet he'd never see.

Amy, however, had wings. Now, though, as she listened to the wind she almost tucked them in and retreated herself. But almost is no place for a pilot, and shuffling through the snow toward the old taildragger she heard the wind change pitch with the muffled clack of a small Continental engine. She squinted at the sound in the winter light and saw wings so slender it was hard to believe they could lift. "Luscombe," she whispered, the way you might say, "Smooth," after sipping a dusky single-malt.

The wind swatted the two-seater, but its pilot paid it no mind. Left aileron up and right one down with rudder urging the airplane's nose straight, the Luscombe touched the runway. Amy tugged her parka's hood tight around her head leaving only a round opening that couldn't hold the smile that drew this visitor toward her. A loose strand of red hair swiped at her face. She tucked it back as the engine quit, and the silver airplane stopped beside her blue Cessna. The two machines rocked wings in greeting while the two human pilots met. "Lost?" Amy called.

"Never," the man from the sky answered as his boots hit the snow making a sound like a fist pressed into corn flakes. He pulled off a black wool cap and ran chapped fingers across thinning hair as dark as his eyes and asked, "You?"

"Can't be lost 'til you quit lookin'," she answered. And his warm smile told her they might take off in formation for nowhere, making this the first Valentine Day ever worth a damn.

© 2006

"Thanksgiving Debonair"

Monterey fog drifted across the bay and stretched for the hills. It coated the tie-down ramp in a film that dripped from trailing edges. The droplets kept beat with the airport's beacon: Green-white…Drip-drip…repeat. Winter meant lean months ahead for flight instructors. Jake would spend more hours staring at the ramp than walking students across it.

There was still an hour until sunset, but the light was dull when Doc's Beech Debonair broke out of the clouds and landed. Its tires barely noted the pavement's existence. Doc taxied toward the hangars giving Jake a friendly wave and then pointed at the gas caps in the universal gesture to bring the fuel truck. With Doc, though, it wasn't a command. Instead, it was: wave first and then request the fuel. For Jake it was an invitation to a corner of the airport where aviation was truly civil. There, conversation was less about "shooting the localizer to minimums" and more about feeling welcome. Doc's airplane reflected her personality and seemed to smile at the other airplanes in passing. Jake wondered if those airplanes were jealous because this one had its own room. But he suspected they'd hide their feelings, because Doc and her Debonair just brought out the best in everyone.

Jake's dog, Leaver—a skinny black collection of muscle and floppy ears like rubber flags—jumped into the cab beside him. A rabbit-chasing, doughnut swiping airport dog, she'd entered his life when it needed a friend. Two years later, she was still there, unlike his ex-wife who'd detested the dog and wasn't too fond of airplanes. "All in all," Jake thought as they pulled beside the Debonair and watched the propeller spin down, "I got the better deal."

Even in twilight, the Debonair glowed. Its yellow finish almost matched the pilot's hair pulled back in a ponytail. And as the door opened with a soft Beechcraft click, she called, "I should give thanks that you're still open. Thought you'd've gone home to a family dinner hours ago."

"Family's with me," Jake replied. "Just another Thursday in November to us." He zeroed the meter and reeled out the hose. Leaver jumped down to wait for Doc to stow Jepp charts and climb out to massage her ears. Jake had a similar fantasy but quietly fueled the airplane.

"Got plans for dinner?"

"Mac and cheese," Jake answered. "With cranberries. You?"

She ignored the question and asked, "So, why do you call her 'Leaver'?"

Jake smiled. "Someone's always tellin' me to leave her behind."

Doc stood. "I hate puns." Then, "Leaver, c'mon, girl, in the backseat!" The dog hopped into the airplane as Doc turned to Jake. "I know a restaurant in Napa. We girls are taking off. If you remember how to read an IFR chart, you're welcome to join us."

Later, Jake glanced at Doc as the Debonair broke through the overcast. Sunset washed across her face, and as corny as it sounded inside his head, he had to say: "Best Thanksgiving ever."

©2007

"Rainy Season's Coming"

Three nights since the last full moon, and Oahu's pre-dawn sky was warm and almost black. Kate met her passenger, Dr. Leo, crossing the ramp muted in dim light. Even in shadow he appeared nervous. Years of flying charter had taught her to spot the difficult ones. So she fired up a smile and called, "Couldn't ask for nicer weather in December!" He hesitated before warning her: "Rainy season's coming."

Kate managed a polite "Yes, but today we'll have a beautiful flight to Molokai." They climbed into her Stinson Junior, and she hurried to start the radial engine in order to flood the cabin with noise so they wouldn't have to talk.

The takeoff was routine after receiving a green light from the control tower. Kate suspected the controller was barely awake at this hour, and, besides, who flew on Sunday? Even with ominous war news from Europe and the far western Pacific, Honolulu on this Sunday morning was comatose. One big hangover trying to sleep until 1942.

The Stinson climbed away from the city lights and headed offshore past the long dead volcanoes at Diamond and Koko Heads. Kate flew east into the trade winds and estimated it would take 23 minutes to cross the Kaiwi Channel. The horizon glowed pink behind Molokai's ridgeback mountain silhouette. A lighthouse waved her around the island's northwestern tip, and she continued along its north shore. Dawn silently displaced night, exposing the Makanalua Peninsula sticking like a dorsal fin into the ocean.

Crumbling surf reached for the dirt runway where the Stinson landed. Kate swung the tail and stopped beside a weathered shack to let Dr. Leo climb out. He stared at the cliffs looming over the Kalaupapa leper colony and, without looking back, reminded her: "Rainy season's coming."

"And aloha to you, too," she muttered and grinned watching him chase his hat tossed by her prop blast when she taxied away.

Kate nearly dipped a wingtip in the water as the long-winged Stinson banked across the shoreline. The ride home was quick with the trade winds and a rising sun on her tail. Oahu floated in the mist before her like a jagged green pillow on blue Jell-O. The sight reaffirmed her decision to move here from Iowa the year before.

Her memories of Midwestern winter flights, though, faded above Waikiki when she noticed several airplane specks over Pearl Harbor. "I'm not the only one working on Sunday," she mumbled and thought it odd. But curiosity quickly turned to fear as smoke billowed in ghostly plumes into the bright sky.

And there were more airplanes. Like hornets. And one—sleeker than anything she'd ever flown—stalked her lumbering Stinson. She marveled at the closure rate and how unreal it looked against the perfect Hawaiian morning. She ducked as it flashed overhead and banked toward her again. In that instant she glimpsed the red blobs on its wings. And, diving for the ground, Kate shivered in the cold realization that "Rainy season's coming...."

©2010

"Solstice Solo"

The December sun retires early at 48 degrees north of the Equator. Not so flight instructors waiting for overdue students to return. Bobby knew he'd goofed. He'd stretched the good fortune of an unusually warm autumn too far. With daylight fading he watched the distant mountaintops obscure in flat clouds. And he swore, more in prayer than a curse at the sky.

"Where'n hell are you?" he asked the stillness that answered with indifference. But even that didn't last. As sunlight faded, the wind took its cue to swoop warrior-like down from the hills. With it came snow—the scratchy kind, stinging its way into any crevice. Bobby pulled his coat tighter and looked back at the flight shack as though by staring at it he could make the telephone ring.

"Hello...where are you?...Good, stay there 'til morning, this is no weather for a student, I shouldn't of let you go...." And he'd hang up before saying he was sorry. But the phone didn't ring. Its bell atop the outside pole silently ignored the cold wind. Bobby listened to snow grains hiss through the wires that crossed the two-lane road and led into town. Eyes lowered, he watched the dry snow swirl across the blacktop. Not long and he'd have to leave.

The sound arrived before the light. Bobby turned toward the east where the muffled clack of the Continental engine sounded oddly confident against the storm. A strobe light pulsed, and then the distinct hello of the Cessna's landing light poked through the gray. The airport's beacon waved back in a green-white flash. His heart beat louder than the wind, and Bobby ran toward the runway. For some reason flight instructors think that if they're a few feet closer to their students in trouble, they can protect them. They'll scare away the monsters and guide them home.

Snow wriggled up his pant leg. It grabbed with needle fingers at his collar, but he didn't mind. Instead, he watched the landing light grow brighter. It seemed to hang there and enlarge rather than get closer, as though becoming a new star. Bobby knew he'd give anything for that star to be safely on the ground. He'd long preached about the glory of flight and had sent this young pilot alone to discover what's beyond the horizon. Now, he felt regret, nudging panic. How could he protect any of them? Who was he kidding? He couldn't bother answering. Instead, he watched the landing light sprout the dim outline of wings. As the light approached earth he saw the pilot's silhouette bobbing inside the airplane. The tires found the dusty runway, and snow curled a powdery wake in the runway lights.

Bobby, the instructor, had to quietly admit, "Nice job." Later, as the Cessna's door opened, his tight throat could only say, "I'm sorry." And his daughter could only ask, "For what?" It was there, in that December night, 48 degrees north of the Equator, that he swore he'd never quit learning.

© 2007

"Freight Dog Holiday"

The last of the solstice orange sunlight filled the cockpit with a blinding smear through a grimy windshield. Pamela squinted while adjusting the visor that snapped off in her hand with a sharp crack. "Piece of..." she muttered and tossed it aside. Since the autopilot had quit an hour back, she'd hand-flown along the airway, amused how Center wouldn't approve her request to go direct. "Unable," the controller replied. "Join Victor 505 and expect the NDB approach." And the depressing phrase, "Radar contact lost," told her she'd have to work for this one.

It was Pamela's annual holiday freight run, but the route was new to her and crossed unfamiliar mountains southwest of the desert high country where she usually flew. Headed into deep canyons, she anticipated the poor radar coverage. Still, it surprised her when fifty miles from her destination ATC lost her below 9000 feet. Unconcerned, she reached for the GPS to program the airway into the box when the screen flickered. "Oh, swell," she hissed, and holding the yoke with her left hand she tapped the GPS face with her right. Sunlight vanished, and turbulence caused her to glance up as cloud tops swept past the airplane. No surprise there. The forecast called for low ceilings and higher tops.

"Freightnight Eleven Eighty-four," Center called through increasing static. "Cross Lyndonville at or above four thousand, cleared approach...altimeter two niner six four." Pressure was dropping faster than expected. She "Wilco'd" the clearance and penetrated dark winter clouds just minutes before the GPS screen flashed dead green. Pamela rarely swore. But alone in the cockpit staring at the blank GPS and facing a hand-flown non-precision approach, she gently invoked the illegitimate offspring of a female dog. Still, in twelve years she hadn't missed a holiday run—they paid too well—so she pushed on. NDB approaches were once routine. "It'll come back," she reassured herself and tuned in the radio beacon. "Remember," she recited, "The ADF needle always tells you where you ain't. If you ain't there, then go there."

Miles later, deep inside freezing clouds, Pamela watched the ADF needle twitch like a drunkard giving directions. It first pointed to the right engine and then to the left until finally toward Lyndonville. Ice slinging off the prop blades cracked like gravel against the fuselage. She'd been through worse, but as she cycled the deice boots and advanced the throttles to hold altitude, she muttered the pilot's prayer, "Just get me through this..." She left any reciprocal promise dangling, because the clouds parted as she completed the procedure turn. The valley floor below was dark except for red and green lights trimming the houses along the two-lane.

Relieved as her wheels touched the slushy runway, she filed that prayer away for another flight. Tonight, she'd offload the cargo into the awaiting delivery truck, swap a "Merry Christmas" with the driver, and then without so much as an "On Piper, on Cessna..." she'd turn around and do it all over again.

© 2008

"Time's Up?"

Climbing through a scattered marine layer, Brent tucked his chin into the fur collar while crouching lower behind the windscreen. Freezing air needled beneath his scarf and behind the rubber cups around his goggles. His eyes watered. His left foot grew achingly cold, and he still had two hours to go before descending into the high desert. Cocooned in a cold muffled roar, he flew behind an engine so hot it would've burned his hands could he have touched it. But none of that heat reached him, and nothing kept him warm. Not the wolverine flying suit, the rabbit-lined mittens or the mukluks on his feet. Not even the biplane's exhaust, flaming yellow against a passing cloud, offered any heat. Although the color told him he was running too rich, so he leaned the mixture to a softer blue. But that only made him feel colder and, yet, content to be untouchable above the earth.

The last of the coastal city lights melted behind the biplane as it cleared the first ridge. Except for a few ranches and occasional headlamps twisting along snowy roads, everything below was empty. He felt suspended in the black sky peppered with stars until the moon popped its half-face above the horizon. Lunar glow smeared the rumpled landscape making the frozen hills look mean. Shadows deepened the canyons and sharpened rocks into bear claws. But despite the lack of suitable emergency landing sites Brent felt comforted by the terrain that was his alone to fear.

He knew the route by heart, having flown it several times a week over the past few years. He missed the summer nights when he'd bounce in soft thermals, inhaling the baked aroma of forest pine and sage in the warm air. And he admitted he'd even miss the winter flights after this mail contract ended at midnight. Taylor Aero Commerce Operations hadn't shown a profit since 1928. And he knew there'd be less call for pilots flying open-cockpit biplanes in an increasingly enclosed sky.

Brent strained to look past the propeller disc for the lighted airway beacons that verified he was on course. Rumor had it that those, too, would be replaced with radio stations, so that pilots wouldn't need to see the landscape to navigate. He questioned whether that was possible or even desirable.

He passed all the lighted beacons on schedule that night, saluting farewell to each in turn. And after clearing the last ridgeline, he throttled back to descend. The distant aerodrome beacon drew the biplane out of the night sky as though to say, "Your time's up, pal."

Twenty minutes later Brent tossed the last bag onto the mail truck. "One minute to midnight," the driver noted before pulling away. Brent stood alone beside a massive structure of wings, struts and useless memories. He removed a flask of bootleg whisky from his flying suit and toasted the biplane. "Happy New Year?"

Wind laughed through the flying wires, convincing Brent that one day he'd feel warm again.

©2010

"Hurry Home"

Seth, 18, couldn't leave campus fast enough. First semester of college done, and he wanted to fly home for Christmas before the weather soured. All morning he'd watched the clouds thicken and sunlight vanish, turning noon into twilight. He brushed snow from the left side of the Piper Pacer's windshield, exposing dead bugs from the last warm-day flight. Oil clung to the dipstick, although, avgas ran freely down his sleeve while sumping fuel tanks that weren't quite full.

Preflight complete, he tossed his books and laundry bag into the baggage compartment and climbed aboard. Calling "Clear prop" to an empty ramp, he pressed the starter button beneath the seat. The Lycoming groaned and then struggled to life with undisguised contempt for the cold. Seth didn't notice. He added power, felt the engine trying to quit and pumped the throttle until the wretched thing agreed to run.

Tumbleweed and snow grains scratched at the gear legs as the Pacer took the runway. Seth leaned slightly forward, his stomach unusually tight. The propeller bit into fat air, and they were barely off the ground when he banked west away from the snow showers moving east. Before him the terrain inclined dramatically toward snow-capped mountains and a wide pass that lead to the valley beyond.

Seth had flown the route so often he'd quit using charts. Despite the overcast, visibility was good as he climbed into the pass above a snaking line of cars along the highway. And as the snake coiled right around a peak, Seth chose to save a few minutes and headed left, where civilization quickly vanished. The mountain ridges below stretched as cold as a dinosaur's smile. The Pacer saw none of this and obediently flew where Seth pointed it. And only Seth saw the overcast sky's belly squeezing them closer to the ground.

Even as visibility diminished he pressed on and was soon skimming the last ridge and descending toward the valley. Warmer air brought light rain and patchy ground fog. When they reached the coastal range, the visibility had dropped to one gray mile. Blindly confident he flew into another familiar pass that led toward home. Bracketed by redwoods so close he could smell them, Seth strained to keep the railroad below in sight but suspected he may have pushed too far.

Who can say what sometimes protects puppies, drunks and young pilots? Certainly Seth didn't question when he saw the coastline and a familiar runway appear in the mist. By now his voice was too tight to use the radio, and he landed without comment. Rainwater washed dead bugs into a smear on the windshield, through which he saw his mother inside the hangar, up to her elbows in a Stinson's engine compartment.

She barely glanced as he taxied to a stop, but her tight Irish stare told him she wasn't pleased. And the motherly dope-slap she administered upside his young head as he approached her reminded Seth there was much that college couldn't teach him.

© 2011

"Uncle Gil's Stinson"

When cold enough, snow acts like sand. Dry and fine, it sifts beneath hangar doors and into dunes around landing gear legs. It hisses to remind you that summer is dead, and spring is frozen deep beneath the grass runway. Gilbert wished global warming would accelerate.

It took an hour to preheat the engine and roll out the Stinson Station Wagon. By then, a familiar Chevy pulled into the parking lot. Gilbert watched his nephew, Ryan, place his good leg outside the car, and then slowly work the other one out. He hesitated after standing, leaning against the car before reaching for his cane. Gilbert pretended not to notice and suppressed the urge to run help.

"Uncle Gil!" Ryan called. "Mom said you'd be out here."

Gilbert pretended to see him for the first time. "I heard you were home for Christmas. Your Dad know you stole his car?"

"He don't mind," Ryan answered and limped around the Stinson, stopping to grab a strut. Gilbert couldn't tell if it was to steady himself or just to reconnect with something from years ago.

"Can I bum a ride?" Ryan asked, and even though he looked all grown up, Gil heard the voice of a kid he used to take flying on summer afternoons. He tried not to stare, but the wind blew Ryan's pant leg, and he glimpsed what the war meant. Titanium and a boot, where once a kid had been. A kid who loved airplanes.

Gil started to speak but felt his voice constrict, and he cleared his throat. "Take the left seat; let's see what you remember."

Ryan slid butt first into the Stinson's cabin, laughing when his boot caught on doorframe. "Still gettin' the hang of all my new hardware."

Gil smiled but wanted to cry, to punch someone who wasn't there. But Ryan didn't give him time and started the engine. The soft rumble of the six-cylinder Franklin isolated their thoughts. Ryan poked his face into the frigid slipstream while listening to the snow crystals hiss past the window. With eyes shut he seemed to inhale the wind. He cracked the throttle and swore gently when, unsteady on the rudder pedals, he taxied through a snowdrift. But his hands knew the yoke and throttle, and his good leg remembered how to hold right rudder in the climb.

In the brief and cold flight Ryan rediscovered his place inside the old airplane. His left turns were uncoordinated, and Gilbert secretly pressed rudder to center the ball. Together, they flew over a town lit for Christmas, around the lake and above memories frozen beneath more than snow. And when the Stinson touched down after sunset, Gilbert wasn't sure what to say other than, "Still landing sideways, ya little twerp."

"Maybe, if the instructor weren't so heavy I'd keep her straight." And it wasn't the same as before. But Uncle Gil vowed that he and the Stinson would be there for as long as this vet needed to return.

© 2009

"The Flight Before Christmas"

Rain swept across Watsonville airport in waves from the low-pressure area stalled northwest of the Monterey Bay. Jake timed them—an hour's soaking followed by a like amount of sunshine. Barely could his shoes begin to dry when someone would call for fuel as the next deluge approached. Then, by late afternoon the airport fell silent, and he sat in the flight school's office beside his dog, Leaver, watching the rain slash at the airplanes on the visitor ramp. It reminded him of small boats in Santa Cruz harbor trying to slip their moorings and drift into the storm.

A Cessna 170 shook off a tiedown rope in a forty-knot gust. Jake scrambled to catch the taildragger before it could free the other wing and tip onto its side. And it was there, miserably soaked to his shorts—his dog loyally observing from the warm office—that Jake decided he was the loneliest pilot in the world on Christmas Eve. Until the other loneliest pilot in the world landed in a crosswind that defied ordinary skill.

Doc was above the ordinary and routinely flew a new 1972 Debonair between the coast and Davis, where she divided her skills among several veterinary clinics. On weekends she'd often fly to the Sierras, and, upon return, Jake would run the old Shell fuel truck to her hangar. There, he'd dawdle longer than needed topping the tanks. Although they were both irreversibly past thirty, Jake felt like an infatuated teen around her. Try as he might he could barely converse on anything other than aviation.

Standing now beneath the Cessna's wing, he hoped to see her signal for fuel. Instead, she waved a friendly no-thanks while taxiing past. "Must have better places to go," he sighed while admiring her profile behind the Debonair's Plexiglas. He cinched the Cessna's wing tight and shuffled through the rain to the office.

Inside, Jake toweled his head with a reasonably clean shop rag, while his shoes steamed atop the propane heater. Leaver slept unruffled by the storm but suddenly sat up with her head cocked and stared toward the front door.

Wind driven rain followed a dark hooded figure into the lobby and rattled the Learn To Fly banner against the wall. Then, before Jake could stammer, "Ghost of Airport Christmas yet to come?" the specter pulled back its hood revealing a face shiny with rain that dripped off her chin.

"So I'm not the only one with nowhere to go tonight," she said. And Jake smiled back as Doc uncapped a thermos bottle and offered: "Cider? It's still hot." Then, as apple and cinnamon vapors loosened their inhibitions, the low-pressure system gradually weakened.

Forty years later the flight school was gone. Passionless self-serve pumps had replaced the fuel truck, and the airport was once again silent as Jake and Doc started their Debonair. And, with Leaver VI in the back seat, the two loneliest pilots in the world shared cider among the stars on another Christmas Eve.

© 2012

"New Year's Resolution"

Every airport has its spiritual guide. Ours was Hal. On December 31st we clustered around him at the FBO's party, awaiting his New Year's resolution. He packed his pipe, lit a wooden match with his thumbnail and through a puff of blue smoke said: "I resolve to fly every day next year." Hal had made the same promise the year before, but five days later his Taylorcraft's engine quit near Salinas, and he landed in an artichoke field. It took almost a year to repair the damage, and he'd never have a nice thing to say about artichokes again. Now, as the calendar flipped a page, Hal's T-craft lifted into a star-clogged sky. His rotating beacon flickered as he passed overhead and turned for the coastline a few miles south.

"A promise made is a debt unpaid," the Yukon poet, Robert Service, wrote, and Hal kept at his New Year's promise to fly every day. When winter storms rolled off the Pacific he'd wait inside his hangar for that pause between the frontal waves. Once the clouds passed, leaving fresh snow on the mountain peak at Loma Prieta, he'd push his airplane into the sunshine. There was always enough time for one lap around the pattern before the rain reappeared. As spring approached and daylight lengthened, Hal would slip into the airport before work to fly for 20 minutes. By summer, he was a minor local celebrity. The newspaper sent a kid reporter who took his picture and asked, "Do you really fly every day?" Hal answered, "Yup." It made for a short Sunday supplement.

Hal flew every day. He'd take off when the fog approached the runway and land before it swallowed the airport whole. He flew when the winds were calm and when they threatened to rip a hangar door from your hand. "Just land across the runway instead of straight down it when the crosswind's that strong," he'd say. "Airplane doesn't know the difference."

By Thanksgiving we sensed the possibility of success, and by Christmas we were ready to anoint him Santa Claus. When another New Year's Eve arrived at the airport so did the crowds to watch our hero fulfill his quest. And we waited. At noon, we searched the ramp. "He isn't anywhere," someone declared, and we all repeated the news. Finally, after dark, Hal drove up and opened his hangar. We clustered around him in the dim light, expecting to see him preflight his airplane for the final triumphant lap. Instead, he removed the airplane's cowling and pulled all the spark plugs. Then, as he opened the oil drain, Thad asked, "It's almost New Year's, Hal. You going to fly?" Hal sat on a toolbox and packed his pipe. He struck a match with his thumbnail and slowly replied, "Nope." And then between puffs of blue philosopher's smoke he added, "Next year." That's when I realized that by attempting to keep his resolution to fly every day, Hal knew that those next years could never end.

© 2007

Chapter 11
The Whole Point of Flight

"Late For Work"

He glanced at his watch—the third time he had done so since leaving the house. The car was pointed toward the freeway, the sun peaking over the trees. Gary turned at the sign reading, AIRPORT. He knew it was wrong.   Dew, from the grass, collected on his shoes. The windsock over the first hangar hung limp, and a sparrow seemed to watch both him and the sunrise. Gary reached for the tiedown rope and untying it, let it fall into the damp grass.

He opened the door. He flicked the master switch, heard the familiar clunk and turned the mag switch to BOTH.

"Clear!" he called to the still dawn. He looked to the sparrow on the windsock. Oil pressure rose quickly and the engine warmed.

Velvet sunlight washed over the runway, and Gary centered the nose on the long green strip.   His hands darted over the familiar controls—mag switch on; fuel on; mixture rich; carb-heat cold.   He inched the throttle forward.   The airplane shook.   Rolling across the uneven surface, the tailwheel bounced in the ruts, the sound echoing through the long fuselage, then the wheels left the ground.

For several minutes it was all there—the sunrise, the calm air, the sky and the feeling that no matter how mundane the rest of the day tried to be, Gary had started above it all.

His approach was smooth.   The wheels touched in gentle rumbles, and he stuck his face through the side window just to watch the tires kick the dew.

In the car, returning to the freeway, he studied the sad, resigned faces around himself, and was glad he was late for work.

© 1989

"Verification"

"I may be mistaken," I said climbing out of the Champ, "but I think that's smooth air up there."

Bill wiped his hands on a rag walking toward the airplane. "Need someone to confirm that, do you?" He tossed the rag near the hangar door.

"Would you?"

He slid into the front seat and fished for the belt. "Switch is off," he called, and I took the propeller in hand. "Brakes are on," he said. "That is if you've ever fixed the silly things."

"Just leave the throttle back," I said. "And make it hot. She'll start." Bill reached behind himself and flipped the mag switch to both. "Hot!" The sixty-five Continental fired on one pull, and I walked away to watch my Champ climb at the sunset.

Golden twilight washed over the wings, and the tires kicked a little dust before lifting from the grass. Bill's turn-out was smooth, low. Banking over the newly plowed fields, I heard him throttle back, just riding the wing, feeling the sky.

He three-pointed it on and taxied to the hangar; the sun had dropped below the tree line, and we were in deep shadow. The propeller took a few easy swings to stop, then he opened the door and set it gently against the rubber stop on the strut.

"Afraid you were right about that," he said. "It's awful smooth up there."

© 1989

"Get Your Mind Off the Ground"

Tailwind. GPS miles ejecting like spent machinegun shells. Pilots love a tailwind, the accomplishment of getting somewhere fast. But if we love flying, why all the rush to end the flight? There's a saying in the Antique Airplane Association: "Almost getting there is half the fun." Don't think about it or you'll make yourself crazy. I did and, well....

Four wings stretched from my body strapped inside a fabric-covered fuselage somewhere over a desert that I'm sure had a name but resembled all the other stretches of sand, rock, and blanched towns I'd crossed for the past few days. Glancing at the GPS strapped to an airframe tube near my right knee, I watched that expanse of Southwest America trickle by in digital bits—no heat, no snakes, no passion for its passing whatsoever, just data saying I'm here, was there, and—because computers can't dream—I'll arrive in exactly this many minutes...now, this many...now, even fewer....

Had I been flying an aluminum tube with a full instrument panel I'd call that progress. An autopilot would free my hands to push buttons and my mind to seek approval from air traffic control before beginning an instrument procedure that would cradle me in government arms from initial to final approach fixes with the assurance that I'd been a good pilot, that I'd managed my cockpit resources well.

Instead, with a hand on the joystick and both feet on the rudder pedals, I looked over an open-cockpit's rim to study the desert below, its sands drifting, salt flats sucking in moisture and time, saying: There was once life here, like yours, but it stopped. So, I kept moving toward a port where a long stretch of pavement with numbers painted on either end oriented my biplane to a faraway magnetic force near Hudson Bay but not to the invisible desert winds that rode bareback down the mountain slopes to push us away from the centerline, to realign us with a runway of its own immense reality, unconcerned with my desires and insulted that I was leaving the sky.

From a couple of thousand feet up in cooler air we had descended into a maw panting hot and merciless closer to an earth most humans knew, the ones, that is, who don't fly. In a sideslip on final with left wings down, right rudder hammered to its stop, the air pressed soft against my face the way flame caresses brick. That same heat forced air molecules apart like a transit cop coaxing New Years drunks to disperse, weakening collective strength until my four wings laced by wires screamed to find lift. Landings were longer in this exhausting world of sun and rock, and arrivals felt like being rescued from a sky that burned on reentry toward the planet's surface. The closer we came to the ground the sky seemed to admonish my decision to leave it with, "Fine, you want down? Here, take your earth, take it hot and in your face." The sky can be such a bitch when you don't clearly communicate: "I need to land; I'm not you."

Humans are so limited. We think we can fly but can't stay aloft without support from below. Avgas for the biplane, water inside an air-conditioned trailer parked on a furnace ramp, and I'd drink to re-inflate after all moisture had been drained from me since climbing toward the sun with nothing above my thoughts except a cloth helmet and the blue so easily confused with heaven. Then, once refueled and as the satisfaction of having arrived faded, I'd feel the urge to leave earth and return again to that sky just above the heat where the only sound was the hymn of the biplane's wings, wires and engine. Where the highways below looked no more significant than a long scratch in time-bleached grit that would one day cover all pretension that dared cross this way.

And because I'm human I'd watch new miles tick away on a GPS calculating progress aligned to a satellite in outer space. Hampered by these data and a mind no larger than one grain of sand I'd trust the human-made stars out there to define my relationship with the billion-year-old mountains below, knowing that the instant I accepted another's advice I'd be lost with too much direction, wondering where my destination really is. For the pilot who views flight as something beyond transportation, the destination gets a bit fuzzy. I don't really want to get there if upon arriving someone will say, "Let's put away your airplane." As in, put away your thoughts for now and take up, again, our ground-based mind.

Beware the forces that draw the pilot downward. Beware the humans who think that air can be conquered, because those are the ones who will clip your dreams.

Alone, in a biplane above a vast expanse of America, the tramp pilot breathes free but only when aloft. To descend, to land and taxi toward civilization is to taxi into snares and nets, to be tied down and, accepting that, to lose lift and stall.

It's the flyer's duty to explode the third dimension and look upward when all others focus on the narrow road ahead. The flyer that taps the sky with a clear eye, will snatch a peripheral vision that so few human beings have ever imagined could be glimpsed. Only the true flyer honest enough to embrace the forces that lift—and, yes, limit—can weave them into the fabric of being itself.

There's no flight plan to clear vision, only the time inside the absence of time above the desert that only you can name. Your vision will be unrelated to anyone else's. Perhaps, your clear mind is already found in the perfect ILS to minimums or inverted at the top of a loop. Only you can fly the route, but it's a surprisingly simple flight to make when you leave the ground to ride the tailwinds already propelling your own mind.

© 2005

"Come Out and Play"

A perfect moment in flight freezes time if you realize the beauty you've experienced. The trick is to make that connection without destroying the illusion.

It was a late summer day filled with bugs in the angled sunlight. I'd just slipped the upper cowling onto the Aeronca Champ's nose when I heard two Continental engines approach from the west. Like kids on bicycles a Cub and a Taylorcraft circled the airfield waiting for me to push out of the hangar and join them to play.

With the tail tied and the wheels chocked, I pulled the prop through to prime the cylinders, then set the magneto switch and throttle, and started the engine. I still get that tiny thrill when hand-propping an old airplane—a bit of danger and awe at the ancient technology that produces flight.

I pulled the chocks, crawled into the cockpit, snapped the seatbelt and, then, reversed the process to climb back out and untie the tail.

Buckled inside again, I cracked the throttle and taxied down the runway through grasshoppers that popped from the dried grass like tiny flying fish.

After a run-up and with the side window open, I took the runway and opened the throttle to create that familiar rumble in the gear legs as the tires bounced through the ruts and ground squirrel holes. Up came the tail, and I squeezed the stick back to ride momentarily in ground effect before brushing the corn at the end of the strip.

Above, the Cub and Taylorcraft waited, and without radios we formed into a loose echelon formation with the Cub in the lead, then at 500 feet we flew southeast across farms ready for harvest and pastures where black cows ignored our passing. We dropped into a river valley to follow the low waters to the Mississippi. Two kids on inner tubes floated in the lazy current, so we circled and waved until they waved back. The Cub descended and touched a wheel on a nearby sandbar; the Taylorcraft followed, and I made the third nick on the sand before we turned away like P-47s after a strafing run on a Rhine barge.

We had no destination, because when you fly old airplanes it's the journey that matters. When a runway appeared it looked all wrong with its PAPIs and instrument touchdown markings, a place for Citations and Bonanzas not for cloth and tube around sky-struck dreamers.

The Cub sidestepped to the right where the last of the summer's hay had been baled into giant green boulders.

Like landing on a chessboard among the pieces we each took a different alleyway between the bales, bounced through coarse stubble, then taxied in-trail to the gas pumps.

Three old tailwheelers on a late summer afternoon—that's all we were, and once we were down, it was gone—the flight now microscopic bits of spent carbon on the breeze. But because it was pure beauty, it's stored in that great vault of flying moments that only those who leave the Earth can understand or find.

© 2001

"Perfect Gift"

"I opened the gate to move the cows from one field to another," he said. "When I heard this motor coming from the sky."

Climbing off the lower wing, I listened to Phillip, who, at eighty-two, had just taken his first open-cockpit, biplane ride, one he'd anticipated since he was twelve. He twisted to undo the shoulder harness and looked past me to another field that, as yet, only he could see.

"There was this airplane like yours, only bigger." He waved faintly at the Marquart Charger's four wings. "And it swooped across the barn to land right where them cows was headed." He pointed to a spot on the horizon seventy years ago, and I turned to see a younger man who'd fought in World War II, had flown as a passenger in airlines, and once in a Cessna. Now, he grasped the upper wing to stand and swing his leg over the cockpit's rim like he'd been doing it his whole life. Suddenly, he was Errol Flynn in Dawn Patrol—a hero from a generation of heroes standing a mile taller than me.

Squinting at the horizon, he continued to develop the memory, "And it rolled to a stop not far from me." He laughed softly. "Oh, them cows run all over the place, but I didn't care because this airplane had just landed in my field." He turned as though offering me something precious that he could no longer carry. "You gotta understand—it was the Depression, and I was a farm kid who'd never seen anything like this, and there it was in my field!"

He climbed down from the wing and gently rubbed my biplane's fuselage the way a farm boy might pat a winning heifer at the county fair, and said, "He never stopped the engine, didn't offer me a ride, just called: 'Which way to Omaha?' So I pointed, and he waved, spun that tail around, and—whoosh! —took off again, scatterin' them cows like old ladies running from a tent preacher."

Phillip waved his arms, and his face went quiet while his mind replayed the scene of the 1930s biplane lifting from his memories.

A half-hour earlier on this day when air travel is common but biplanes rarely drop into normal lives, Phillip had struggled to pull himself up the wings and bend stiff joints into the front seat. He'd waved apprehensively to his daughter who took digital pictures, and, before takeoff, I caught a what-the-hell-am-I-doing-here? look in his profile.

But after twenty minutes in the warm summer morning, floating above trees, lakes, and a cow pasture where he looked down at a farmer opening a gate from one field to another, I suspected this biplane ride from a daughter to a Dad who'd told her many times about that winged visitor, was the perfect gift and long overdue.

As they walked away I touched the flying wires and wondered what I was supposed to do with that gift Phillip had left behind.

© 2005

"Brickyard"

The river wound south of the city through woods and a clearing full of dead automobiles. The air was smooth and the sky clear but for a few spent clouds floating above like party balloons against the ceiling. In the Aeronca Champ, I've spent most of my flying life looking up at clouds. Sure, I've seen them from the tops and flown through on the gauges in other airplanes, but the best slot is several hundred feet above the trees where on hot days you can smell the earth through an open window.

This day was cool, and the leaves below knew it was autumn. They didn't complain the way humans do about the inevitability of winter and ice. Instead, they dropped like cheap foreign money into the river and by doing so, exposed a piece of history that, on the sectional chart, was merely labeled "Brickyard."

I'd flown across this stretch before, but always higher and faster while pointed at some GPS waypoint like a birddog on a pheasant. But, now, at 500 feet I looked down at what had once been a large brick factory. Apparently, the demand for bricks died one day and everyone went home, the kiln fires cooled, and the railroad cars pulled away never to return. Located far from the main highway, no one saw the woods slowly overtake what bricks had been left on pallets in a dusty yard.

Fascinated, I circled this lost city and with each pass, layers of time peeled away exposing the generations. I saw the ghosts of workers in rough clothes and could imagine square cars with running boards parked by the main entrance in a now deserted lot. An entire industrial life unfolded beneath me from start to finish.

Airplanes allow us to see things that others can't. This tiny corner of the Midwest had once flourished and then by whatever power decides that farms should be malls and runways become cul-de-sacs, a brick factory had died like the last dinosaur inside a hidden valley. In time its cold chimneys would topple, and the corrugated sheds would blow away in a spring thunderstorm. Alone, it would vanish and no one would know or care.

We like to save things—postcards, whales, rain forests. We save cathedrals without saints, train stations where the tracks no longer run, and we save old airplanes often knowing they'll never fly again.

We can't stop time, not if we insist upon living by it. When restoring the past, our inclination is to make it prettier than new and lock it inside a museum encircled by a velvet rope to show that it's special and shouldn't be touched.

But some old airplanes are meant to fly and would only wilt in the fluorescent light and conditioned air of a museum. They need sunlight and dust and the smell of autumn through the window. In return for this chance to live, old airplanes will show you where memories lie moldering in the woods. Then, once you take the time to circle and hear the stories, you'll become an aviation archeologist and unearth the endless treasures waiting beneath your wings.

© 2001

Time for your Aeromancy journal to begin. Write your stories on the following pages and share with your friends or enemies...whatever works.

-Paul Berge